ABDELLATIF RAJI

Where the World Forgets

www.yeraak.com

First edition

ISBN (paperback): 978-1-963876-67-3
ISBN (hardcover): 978-1-963876-66-6
ISBN (digital): 978-1-963876-65-9

This book was professionally typeset by Yaraak.
Find out more at yaraak.com

For the ones who remember.
For the ones who can't.
And for all those who carry the stories of others in their hearts—
even when the world tries to silence them.
This is for you.

"The struggle of memory against forgetting is the struggle of humanity against power."

— MILAN KUNDERA

Contents

Foreword

When I first began writing *Where the World Forgets*, it wasn't meant to be a story about memory. Not exactly. It began as a question: **What happens when the truth is too heavy to carry—and too dangerous to forget?**

But as the pages unfolded, I found myself returning, again and again, to the fragile beauty of remembrance. To the idea that memory is not just an archive of the past, but a compass for the future. That in every story we tell—especially the painful ones—we stitch ourselves back together.

This book was born from the quiet fears we don't always speak aloud: the fear of losing someone we love to time, to silence, to a world that changes too fast. It was also born from hope—the kind that smolders even when everything seems lost.

Mira's journey is one of truth, sacrifice, and resilience. She is not a superhero. She is not perfect. She is *us*—flawed, grieving, afraid. And still, she chooses to fight for something bigger than herself. Her courage reminds me, and I hope reminds you, that even in dystopian shadows, a single voice can carry the dawn.

Thank you for opening this book.

Thank you for remembering.

— Abdellatif Raji

Preface

In a world increasingly saturated with noise, distraction, and misinformation, memory has become more than just a personal record—it is an act of resistance. *Where the World Forgets* was written in response to the quiet erasures we witness every day: the silencing of histories, the rewriting of truths, and the fading of shared understanding.

This story is set in a future twisted by climate catastrophe and authoritarian control, but its roots lie deeply in our present. What happens when survival comes at the cost of identity? What do we sacrifice in the name of order? And most of all, what remains when everything else is stripped away?

At its core, this book is about **what we choose to remember**—and why it matters.

Through Mira's journey, I wanted to explore not just the trauma of forgetting, but the profound courage it takes to hold onto love, truth, and self in a world built to erase them. Her defiance, her compassion, and her losses are reflections of countless unnamed struggles unfolding across our own world today.

This book doesn't promise easy answers. But it dares to ask difficult questions. And it offers this: that memory—however fractured—is still one of humanity's most powerful tools for healing, for justice, and for change.

May you read this story not only as fiction, but as a reminder.

Of what must never be forgotten. Of what we are capable of remembering—together.

— Abdellatif Raji

Acknowledgments

This story, like memory itself, is a mosaic—shaped by many hands, hearts, and histories. It would not exist without the people who helped me remember who I am, and why stories matter.

To my family—thank you for grounding me in love, even when the world felt like it was unraveling. Your voices are the lullabies that live inside these pages.

To the friends who read early drafts, offered honest feedback, or simply reminded me to keep going—your belief meant more than you know. You helped me find my courage when mine flickered.

To the scientists, climate advocates, and mental health professionals whose work inspired so many elements of this novel—thank you for fighting daily battles against forgetfulness, denial, and despair.

To the unnamed, forgotten, or erased voices throughout history—this book is for you. May we continue to remember you, speak your names, and carry your truths forward.

To my readers—thank you for choosing to spend time in this world I created. Thank you for holding space for Mira, for Lena, for the broken and brave.

And finally, to the storytellers who came before me, and those still to come:

Never stop writing into the silence.

Never stop remembering.
With deepest gratitude,
— Abdellatif Raji

Prologue

The city used to remember.

Its streets once echoed with laughter, protest chants, whispered stories passed between generations. Windows glowed with late-night reading lights. Names meant something. Faces held histories.

Now? The city sleeps with one eye open, and its people walk like ghosts.

They do not remember the flood that swallowed the harbor.

They do not remember the first child who forgot her mother's name.

They do not remember how the sky changed.

But Mira Solis remembers.

She remembers the weight of her father's hand slipping from hers the day he forgot who she was.

She remembers the last time her sister said "I love you" and meant it.

She remembers the silence that followed the truth's burial—and the aching emptiness it left behind.

Most of all, she remembers the moment she chose to fight.

Not because she wasn't afraid.

But because she was. Because the forgetting had stolen too much. Because someone had to remember, and if not her—then who?

In the stillness before the storm, with smoke curling from the broken skyline and memories falling like ash, Mira stood in the shadows of a world that wanted her quiet and chose instead to *speak*.

This is not a story of perfect heroes.

It is the story of what happens when a single voice dares to rise.

When memory, long-buried, becomes fire.

And when the sky—finally—begins to remember.

Introduction

Where the World Forgets is a story about memory—not just the kind stored in brains or books, but the kind etched into our relationships, our choices, our courage. It's a tale of resistance set in a broken world, but it was born from very real fears: environmental collapse, authoritarian control, and the quiet erosion of truth.

This book isn't meant to predict the future—it's meant to *warn*, and to *inspire*.

Through the eyes of Mira Solis, we follow not a superhero, but a young woman carrying unbearable grief and impossible hope. Her journey is one of reclaiming stories stolen by silence, of choosing truth when lies are safer, and of learning that memory—no matter how fragile—is the beginning of justice.

At its core, this is a love letter to remembrance.

It honors those who refuse to forget, who preserve names and voices against the tide of erasure. It asks: What are we, if not the sum of what we've seen, loved, lost, and chosen to keep alive?

If you've ever felt afraid of forgetting, or of being forgotten… this book is for you.

Let it remind you that remembering is resistance.

And that even in the darkest hour, *truth still rises*.

1

Drowned World

The air reeked of salt, sewage, and slow decay—a humid, chemical rot that clung to the lungs and never fully let go.

Mira Solis pulled her hood tighter, squinting against the wind that carried flecks of briny mist from the encroaching sea. Her boots slapped against the pavement, soles worn smooth from walking the same ruined blocks day after day. As she stepped into the ration line, her eyes scanned the hunched figures ahead—neighbors, strangers, survivors. No one met her gaze.

Above them, the sky sagged with clouds like bruises. New Harbor City—once New York—stood like a drowning giant, its bones rusting, its glass skin shattered and weeping. The seawalls moaned beneath the pressure of rising tidewater, ancient concrete and steel groaning with each passing wave. In the distance, the ocean lapped hungrily at a half-sunken cruise ship, its rusted hull wedged between collapsed skyscrapers like a forgotten monument to excess.

Here, in the lower sectors, survival came in hours. Not days.

Not weeks. Just moments measured by breath and memory.

The line crept forward, weaving past shattered storefronts, broken streetlamps, and makeshift barricades built from sheet metal and prayer. They passed what had once been a plaza, now dominated by a twisted statue of Liberty holding not a torch, but a purification canister—issued by the Authority after the first wave of neurotoxin leaks. Her face, pocked with mold and bird droppings, had long since lost its hopeful gaze.

Mira shifted her satchel on her shoulder, feeling the familiar lump of a waterlogged paperback inside. She brushed its frayed corner with her fingertips, grounding herself. It was the only kind of memory she trusted anymore.

Overhead, a low *vrrmm* made the crowd freeze. Mira's head tilted just enough to see a surveillance drone gliding along the wind, a silent predator with blinking blue eyes. Its undercarriage hummed with energy—scanners sweeping across the line like a thousand invisible hands.

Everyone tensed. No one moved.

Then came the chirp.

"IDENTITY CHECK IN PROGRESS: CITIZEN ROLAND VERA. ANOMALY DETECTED."

Roland—a wiry man with hollow cheeks and calloused hands—went pale. His eyes darted from face to face, sweat beading on his brow despite the cold.

"I—I'm Roland," he stammered. "Roland Vera. I know my number. I do. Just give me a moment—"

The drone hovered lower, casting a red beam onto his chest like a target.

"NON-COMPLIANT DATA. CITIZEN TO BE ES-CORTED FOR HEALTH EVALUATION."

From a shadowed archway, two Authority enforcers stepped

forward—black exo-suits gleaming, visors blank, movements machine-precise. Roland backed away instinctively, hands raised.

"Please," he begged, his voice cracking. "I just forgot one number. Just one."

His gaze landed on Mira—desperate, pleading, human.

Something in her snapped.

She stepped forward, her voice low but steady. "Three-two-nine-four-five-six. That's the number you gave me. When you fixed the water filter. Remember?"

Roland's lips moved in stunned silence. Then:

"Three-two-nine-four-five-six," he repeated, louder now. "Roland Vera. ID Three-Two-Nine-Four-Five-Six."

The drone paused. A flicker of processing.

Mira held her breath.

"**ERROR OVERRIDE DENIED. CITIZEN ESCORTED PER DIRECTIVE 14-B.**"

The enforcers advanced. Mira stepped back quickly, heart pounding. Roland didn't resist as they seized his arms. He looked over his shoulder one last time, not at Mira, not at the drone, but at something far beyond them.

"Don't forget," he murmured. "Please… someone remember."

They vanished into a side street swallowed by shadow.

Mira exhaled, fists clenched at her sides.

They always called it a health evaluation.

But no one came back.

The line shuffled forward again. No one spoke. No one looked at her. Fear lived in the spaces between them, thick as the mist.

Ten minutes later, Mira reached the distribution point—a rusting metal table manned by a bored-looking Authority worker behind reinforced plex. He slid her a dented canister with "POTABLE – CLASS B" stamped across the side. She didn't speak. Neither did he.

She turned toward home, the water heavy in her pack, her thoughts heavier still.

The streets shimmered with oil-slick puddles and jagged reflections. Rainwater pooled in old gutters, carrying flakes of rust and filth like confetti. As she passed the seawall, a towering billboard sparked to life above her. Its glow flickered through the haze.

"TRUST THE VOICE OF STABILITY. THE FORGET-TING IS UNDER CONTROL. STAY CALM. STAY COM-PLIANT."

The screen shifted.

Minister Celeste Drake's face filled the city's view—her expression perfectly sculpted: warm eyes, smooth skin, a voice that could lull you into surrender. She looked serene, powerful, untouchable.

Mira turned away before her rage could catch fire.

By the time she reached her apartment block—a sagging monolith perched just above the waterline—her shoulders throbbed and her knees ached. She keyed in the entry code, passed through the aging security scanner, and began the climb. Elevators hadn't worked since the blackout last summer, and no one expected them to again.

Her unit on the sixth floor was dry, barely. The scent of mildew greeted her like an old friend. She dropped her satchel with a thunk, peeled off her coat, and crossed to the corner where her shelves stood like sentinels.

Her archive.

Worn books stacked two, sometimes three rows deep. Paperbacks swollen from rain. Spines cracked open like ribs. She didn't care. These weren't just stories. They were *truths* no one could erase. Real, tangible memory in a world where everything else could be rewritten or deleted with a keystroke.

She pulled out the latest addition: a battered copy of *The Little Prince*, its pages warped, the ink running in places like melted dreams. She cradled it like a living thing, pressing her fingers to the smudged cover.

Outside, sirens shrieked again.

A drone buzzed past her window.

And somewhere—just a few blocks away—another person's name vanished from the ledger of the living.

Mira clutched the book to her chest and whispered into the gloom, "Don't forget."

The words were small. Powerless, maybe.

But they were hers.

And for now, they were enough.

2

Fragments of Home

Ｔhe apartment smelled faintly of old paper, steamed rice, and salt—like history trying to simmer in a pot barely warm. Mira could count the grains left in the storage tin on one hand. She didn't need to count, really. She already knew. That kind of scarcity became muscle memory.

She moved quietly, her footsteps muffled against the peeling linoleum, not wanting to wake Lena just yet. The morning light filtered through layers of soot and condensation, casting pale ribbons across the walls like faded sunbeams caught in smoke. The windowpanes rattled gently in the breeze—a sound she'd grown so used to, she barely noticed.

Mira stood before the shelf in their shared room, a place she treated with the same reverence others gave to altars. Her fingers drifted along warped spines and melted bindings. A photo album with curling edges. A tangle of diaries tied together with scavenged twine. A broken fountain pen. And there, nestled between two old history books, her father's notebook—leather cracked and softened with time, his initials *C.S.* still visible in careful, looping script.

This wasn't just a collection. This was her fortress. A defense against the world's vanishing. When the city outside grew too quiet, too still—like it was holding its breath—these objects whispered back. Anchors in the drift.

Some nights she read the same passages over and over, as if the repetition might pin her to the past like a thumbtack to a map. Some days she couldn't bear to open a single page, afraid that even the memory of remembering would fade.

Behind her, a voice rasped through sleep. "You're up early."

Mira turned. Lena sat upright in bed, hair sticking out in all directions like a dark halo, her face half-shadowed by the blanket still clutched to her chest.

"I'm always up early," Mira said, smiling softly. "You just like to pretend you don't notice."

Lena squinted at her. "I notice. Sometimes."

Mira crossed the room and bent to kiss her sister's forehead. The scent of lavender still clung to her—faint, but present— thanks to a sachet Mira had traded for at the market. It reminded her of their mother, and that alone made it priceless.

"Get up," she said, tapping Lena's knee. "Before breakfast evaporates."

They gathered at their tiny folding table, knees pressed together beneath a fraying quilt that doubled as a curtain, wall-hanging, and emergency blanket. Mira ladled out rice porridge—thin as memory, more water than meal—with a sliver of seaweed for garnish.

Lena stared at her bowl. "Let me guess. Chef's special?"

"Gourmet rations," Mira said, lifting her spoon like a toast. "Ocean-aged to perfection. With hints of iodine and survival."

Lena rolled her eyes. "Aged in despair."

Mira laughed, and Lena joined her, the sound sudden and

sharp and so utterly *human* that it took Mira's breath away. She closed her eyes for a heartbeat, imprinting the moment in her mind. If she could store that laugh somewhere safe—on a shelf, in a page, in a breath—she would.

As they ate, Mira reached into her satchel and pulled out a small, flattened foil wrapper. Purple. Torn neatly at one side, the scent almost gone.

"What's that?" Lena asked, curious.

"Chocolate," Mira said reverently. "Or at least, it *was*. I found this yesterday in the market. Just the wrapper, but—when I smelled it? I remembered everything. The way it melted on your tongue. That one birthday with the cake. Remember?"

Lena leaned in, sniffed it, then sat back. Her brow furrowed, the way it always did when her brain was working hard.

"I… I think I do," she said. "There was a candle. You lit it. I forgot the wish."

Mira nodded, masking the ache behind her smile. "That's okay. I remember it for both of us."

They finished breakfast in quiet—comfortable, but weighted. The kind of silence that wasn't absence, but **effort**. Like both were pretending not to see the frayed edges pulling free.

After clearing the table, Mira spread a makeshift worksheet in front of Lena: scraps of scavenged paper with smudged lines, a pencil worn down to its core.

"Quiz time," she said, too cheerfully.

Lena groaned. "Miraaa."

"You don't get out of learning just because the world's ending. Education is rebellion."

"You sound like Dad."

"I'm taking that as a compliment."

Lena puffed her cheeks and slouched. "Fine. Ask."

"Who was the last elected president before the Unity Authority?"

Lena's eyes darted left, then up, then narrowed as if trying to pull the name from smoke. "It was… um… I *know* this. It was…"

The pencil slipped from her fingers. Her face twisted with frustration.

"I *knew* this yesterday," she whispered. "Why can't I—why does it just go *blank*?"

Mira's heart clenched. She reached out, took Lena's trembling hands in hers.

"It's okay," she said softly. "You're okay."

"No, I'm not!" Lena snapped, wiping at her eyes. "What if I forget you? What if I wake up one day and I don't know your name?"

Mira's throat tightened. She fought the panic. She couldn't afford it. Not in front of her sister.

"You won't," she whispered. "Not while I'm here. I'll be your memory, if I have to. I'll write you stories, draw you maps, tell you our secrets again and again. I'll *never* let you forget."

Lena collapsed into her arms. They sat like that a long time— two girls against a tide trying to erase them.

Later, while Lena slept curled beside the heater clutching a ragged bear, Mira returned to the archive.

She pulled her father's journal from the shelf and opened to a ribbon-marked page.

March 19. She asked me why the stars don't shine anymore. I told her the sky was just hiding. I didn't have the heart to say I think they're gone.

Mira traced the ink, rough and faded, but still there. Still *his*.

Dr. Carlo Solis had once been one of the brightest minds in

the city—a memory specialist, a scientist who believed memory could heal societies. The irony that he'd been one of the first to succumb to the Forgetting was not lost on her.

She had watched him unravel. Names, dates, faces—each one slipping like beads from a broken thread. Until the day he looked at her and asked if she was one of the nurses.

He died months later, alone and blank.

Their mother had gone even earlier—ripped from them in a flash flood that swallowed half the southern city. Mira still dreamt of that day. Of reaching, screaming, falling short. Of drowning in more than just water.

She closed the journal and clutched it to her chest.

She would not forget. Not them. Not their voices. Not who they were before.

Outside, the wind rose, keening through broken window-panes. Distant sirens echoed like hollow bells. Somewhere, another name was being lost.

Inside, Mira lit a stub of wax, curled into the corner, and opened the photo album.

This was her ritual. Her vow.

Each page, each note, each whispered word…

A rebellion against oblivion.

3

A Spark of Suspicion

The hum of the scanners was the closest thing to music in the Central Records Depot. That, and the faint clatter of keyboards, the sigh of overworked ventilation, and the endless shuffle of paper that had long since outlived its purpose.

Mira sat in her assigned pod, enclosed on three sides by frosted glass. Beyond, a sterile sea of workstations stretched beneath flickering fluorescent strips, and above, a spiderweb of vents exhaled cold, filtered air that smelled like dust and bleach. The depot wasn't meant to inspire comfort—it was meant to *erase noise*, reduce identity. Just another node in the Authority's great forgetting machine.

Rows upon rows of reinforced metal shelves rose in every direction like a fossilized forest. Each one housed brittle manila folders, reel cartridges, and matte-gray data slates stamped with the Unity Authority's sigil—a closed eye encircled by a crown of stars. Surveillance in metaphor. Surveillance in law.

Mira adjusted the latex-thin gloves they were all required to wear, ostensibly for "preservation integrity," though everyone knew they were more about preventing physical contact with forbidden knowledge. She slid a yellowed page into the digitizer tray. The machine blinked twice before whirring to life.

January 23, 2037: Tens of thousands gather in coastal cities to protest the SkyShield deployment—

A pause. Then a thick black bar swallowed the line whole.

Mira exhaled sharply through her nose.

She continued scrolling, but the rest was the same. More redactions. More blackouts. Photographs with faces blurred beyond recognition. Reports with entire paragraphs excised. Protest leaders listed as "citizen anomalies." Casualties described as "incidents concluded." Truth stripped and rewoven into state-approved fabrications.

That morning, her supervisor—Halden, M., all vinegar breath and bureaucratic disdain—had sauntered into her pod, arms loaded with a fresh batch of deletion orders.

"Protest logs, pre-Authority era," he'd said, like someone casually announcing a menu change. "We're streamlining. All that fearmongering from the Old Times is emotionally destabilizing."

"They're historical documents," Mira had murmured, careful to keep her tone neutral.

Halden had not even looked up from his clipboard. "They're clutter. Sentiment makes for sloppy records."

Now she stared down at a black-and-white photograph queued for deletion. A woman with wild hair shouting into a megaphone, her face contorted in righteous fury. Around her stood children—fists raised, faces fierce—holding handmade signs: *WE REMEMBER.*

Something in Mira's chest twisted.

She hovered her cursor over the "Delete" command.

Then moved it.

With a quick tap, she flagged the image for internal archive only—secretly saving it to an encrypted personal drive she'd hidden three directories deep. It was against protocol, but so was *breathing too loud* in this place.

A small act of rebellion. A whisper of resistance.

It wasn't much.

But it was something.

She was about to move on when the sound of footsteps broke her focus—irregular, hesitant, far too slow for anyone on official business. They scraped, not clicked.

Mira glanced up.

"...Mira..."

The voice was papery and familiar, worn down by wind and time. It slid into her ears like a forgotten melody.

Her heart stuttered.

"Professor Malik?" she breathed.

The figure approaching her station looked like a shadow of the man she remembered. His coat hung loosely from his frame, more bones than body, and his hair—once salt and pepper—was now snowy and thin. His eyes were cloudy, but they fixed on her like she was the last anchor in a sea of dissolution.

"Mira Solis," he said, each syllable like a cracked stone. "You look... just like him."

She stood up, glancing nervously toward the drone mounted in the ceiling corner, its blue light pulsing faintly.

"Professor, how did you get in here? This area's restricted."

"I was looking," he said, voice trembling. "For the real pages. Carlo said they were here. He promised."

Carlo. Her father.

Mira's pulse jumped.

People were starting to notice. Archive assistants had paused mid-keystroke. A few turned in their chairs. Even the overhead drone had angled slightly in their direction, blinking red.

Mira moved swiftly, stepping out from her pod. "Let's talk in the reading alcove," she said, gently taking his elbow.

He didn't resist. In fact, he clung to her with startling strength.

They moved to a quieter corner, a wedge of the depot carved out for rare consultations and overlooked files. The walls there were lower, the cameras fewer.

Malik sank onto a bench with a sigh. His hands fluttered over his knees. "Carlo knew," he whispered. "The Forgetting… it's not disease. It's consequence."

Mira crouched beside him. "Tell me everything."

"They said it was natural," he continued, eyes unfocused. "Memory loss, cognitive drift. Climate stress. But it started right after SkyShield went live. Carlo tracked the correlation. The particles. The exposure zones. It wasn't a coincidence. It wasn't random."

Her breath caught. "SkyShield?" she echoed. "The climate shield program?"

He nodded slowly. "Project SkyShield. Launched 2035. Injected aerosol particulates to cool the upper atmosphere. Effective at first. Too effective. But they lied about the side effects. Neuro-disruption. Memory decay. Carlo tried to sound the alarm. They buried him instead."

The world tilted.

"I thought he was paranoid," Malik murmured, eyes flickering. "But then I began to forget, too. I saw the patterns. I saw the… the spread. The Vault, he said. The real files. He hid them before they could destroy the truth."

"What vault?" Mira whispered.

17

He looked at her, clarity piercing through the fog like sunlight through clouds. "He said you might find it. That you'd be the one. That you'd remember what he couldn't."

Then he reached into his coat and pressed something into her hand.

A key. Cold. Rusted. Small.

Its teeth were worn smooth, the head stamped with a faded code she didn't recognize.

"Before they make us forget again," he whispered. "Remember."

And then chaos.

Two security officers rounded the corner, flanked by a sharp-faced woman in a Memory Services coat. Her eyes flicked from Mira to Malik.

"There he is," she said. "Professor Malik, your group therapy is waiting."

Mira stood protectively, placing herself between them. "He's not dangerous," she said quickly. "He's confused. He's sick."

The woman offered a tired, professional smile. "We know. That's why we're here."

As they led him away, Malik twisted in their grasp. His gaze found Mira one last time.

"Remember," he said again, voice ragged. *"Remember what they want to bury."*

Then he was gone.

Mira stood there, her hand clenched around the key, its edges biting into her palm.

The depot buzzed as before. Screens flickered. Workers resumed typing, like nothing had happened.

But something had changed.

Mira's chair felt too small. Her workstation too exposed. The walls too thin. Every shadow now had shape.

Outside the depot's high windows, the billboard flickered to life. Celeste Drake's face glowed over the cityscape, her voice honey-smooth and iron-hard:

"Spreading misinformation about the Forgetting is a threat to social cohesion.

Truth is memory. Trust the Authority."

Mira didn't look away.

Her reflection stared back at her, distorted in the glass, and she didn't recognize the expression on her own face.

Something between fear... and awakening.

She pressed her hand to her pocket.

The key was still there.

And suddenly, the archive—her sanctuary, her second home— felt less like a vault of history and more like a cage.

They had buried the truth.

And now... she was going to dig.

4

The Vault of Memories

The city curled itself into shadow as curfew fell, sirens howling once like wolves before dissolving into the electric hush of a silenced population. New Harbor's veins emptied beneath the amber glow of faltering streetlights, while flickering surveillance drones zipped over rooftops like moths drawn to movement. The tide crept over cracked pavement below, gurgling against the seawalls. Mira stood at the window, her breath fogging the glass as she watched the skies. The old blackout curtains were drawn just wide enough for her to track the patterns of light above—searchlights, drones, distant flashes of rain reflecting off the ruined skyline.

Behind her, Lena snored softly, curled into a crescent of frayed blankets. One arm clutched her oldest companion: a stuffed bear missing one button eye. Mira smiled faintly at the sight. The bear had survived more than most people they knew. It, at least, still remembered what comfort felt like.

Mira's hand slipped into her coat pocket and closed around the small, rusted key.

Its weight was disproportionate to its size, as though it carried gravity itself.

The image of Professor Malik's trembling hand, the urgency in his eyes, his voice—"Before they make us forget again"—still echoed in her mind like a whisper through a locked door.

She couldn't ignore it.

She wouldn't.

Slipping out of the apartment, she moved like smoke—silent, careful, fluid. The door closed behind her with a soft *click*, a final breath before descent. The city held its breath, too. Mira could feel it in the stillness—an eerie quiet that pressed against her ears like pressure beneath water. The hush of fear, of submission, of people trying not to be noticed.

Her route was instinctual. Past the crumbling façade of the old theatre, whose marquis still blinked "NOW SHOWING: TRUST" in flickering red letters. Through a gap in the alley beside the ration center, where rats fled from puddles of brackish water. Down a ladder into the old canal tunnels, long abandoned, their purpose buried under sediment and secrets. There, the air smelled of rust, algae, and forgotten things.

Mira moved quickly. The tunnels whispered with echoes of history. Graffiti from decades past bled through layers of grime—memorials, protests, names of the lost. She ran her fingers over one faded phrase:

THE TRUTH SLEEPS BELOW.

The words settled in her bones.

The Central Records Depot rose ahead like a fortress carved from stone and shadow. A relic of bureaucracy, its bulk hunched beneath the skeletons of collapsed buildings. Most entered through the main gates under biometric surveillance. Mira crept instead to the back, through a path overgrown with creeping ivy and tangled wires, where the old freight hatch slumped against the concrete wall.

She knelt before the padlock. Hands shaking, she slid the key into place.

It turned.

The lock groaned like something ancient waking from a long slumber. The hatch creaked open, spilling dust and damp air from the black beyond.

Mira slipped inside.

The air was thick and cool. She descended a spiral of iron steps, her flashlight cutting through cobwebs that drifted like strands of memory. The scent of ozone, mildew, and something metallic filled her nostrils. Each footstep echoed up into the dark above, swallowed by silence.

The basement level wasn't on any active floor plans. Mira only knew of it from her father's old scribbles—half-legible diagrams and cryptic notes buried among his journals. "The place they won't look," he'd once written. "Where we keep what matters."

When she reached the bottom, her light revealed a corridor clogged with old shelving units, collapsed crates, and filing cabinets left to rust. Dust coated everything like snow. Some bulbs overhead still clung to life, flickering feebly like stars refusing to die. Mira moved carefully, ducking under sagging ceiling panels and past collapsed ceiling tiles.

Then she saw it.

A rusting vault door at the far end of the corridor, ringed in flaking paint and crowned with an ancient keypad blinking red. The final threshold.

She approached, fingers gripping the key like a lifeline.

The lockplate beneath the console was nearly invisible, hidden behind a sliding panel. She inserted the key. Turned.

Click.

The panel blinked green.

With a groaning shudder, the door unlatched and eased open.

The breath Mira had been holding finally escaped.

The Vault was real.

And it was waiting.

Inside, time stood still. The air was thick with stillness, the kind that accumulates in sacred spaces. Metal filing cabinets lined the walls, each labeled by hand. Paper sat in neat piles—some wrapped in string, others slid into protective sleeves. Dozens of data drives sat stacked in drawers, alongside notebooks, cassette tapes, and even a box of old flash drives labeled with color-coded tabs.

Mira crossed the room slowly. She brushed her hand against a drawer, leaving a trail in the dust. Her flashlight landed on a corkboard hung with photos, maps, graphs, and notecards. Every word written in the same careful script: her father's.

Tears pricked her eyes.

He'd built this. In secret. For the day when someone might need to remember.

She opened the nearest file:

April 3, 2035 – Initial cases of short-term memory collapse in test zones. Unexplained. Report suppressed.

May 19, 2035 – Neurological disruptions observed in lab animals exposed to aerosol compounds.

June 7, 2035 – Project SkyShield internal memo: "Public exposure risks unacknowledged. Recommend suppression."

SkyShield. Over and over.

A climate intervention turned neurological catastrophe. A solution that turned poison. And the government had known.

She pulled out a red-stamped document labeled: **CON-FIDENTIAL – EYES ONLY**. Inside was a memo from the Ministry of Environmental Advancement:

"Observed side effects in atmospheric test zones include disorientation, memory loss, and cognitive fragmentation. Civilian exposure in metropolitan regions exceeds projected thresholds. Media blackout protocols engaged. Recommend concealment of side-effect data until sociopolitical stability is secured."

Mira's stomach churned.

They knew.

They *chose* this.

Her flashlight flickered. She turned and saw a small terminal on a desk in the corner, dust covering its keyboard like a veil. One data drive blinked with a slow, steady pulse—like a heartbeat.

She inserted it and pressed PLAY.

Her father's voice came through, raw and distant.

"Mira… if you're hearing this, it means I've failed. Or worse… I've been made to forget."

Mira's breath caught.

"The memory loss—it started right after SkyShield. That wasn't an accident. They knew. They didn't finish testing. They let it go global anyway. Said it was worth it. Celeste knew. She ordered the redactions. Said the panic would be worse than the sickness. I tried to stop it. They silenced the team… I had to hide the truth."

"Elena Alvarez... she was the only one who walked away. She has the missing data. She knew it was wrong. Find her. Trust no one else. And Mira... I'm sorry I left you this way."

The recording ended with a faint, broken breath.

Mira sat motionless, her hand trembling on the keyboard.

Her father hadn't forgotten her.

He'd remembered enough to leave her the truth.

She packed everything she could: the memo, the SkyShield files, the data drive. She shoved them into her satchel, pulse racing.

Then—*ping.*

A sharp, mechanical tone echoed through the corridor. A motion sensor. The light near the stairs turned red.

Voices above. Footsteps descending.

They know.

She snatched the flashlight and sprinted to the opposite wall. Her fingers found a loose panel—an emergency maintenance hatch once used by janitors. She squeezed through just as heavy boots clanged down the stairwell behind her.

Her satchel thumped against her ribs as she ran. Dust rained from the ceiling. Her lungs burned.

She emerged into the night, gasping, the alley behind the depot slick with rain.

Searchlights scanned the streets.

She didn't stop.

Down an alley. Over a wire fence. Past garbage fires and silent witnesses. She didn't stop until she found the old train underpass and collapsed beneath it, soaked and shaking.

Her father had left her the truth.

And now, the lie was chasing her.

Mira curled around the satchel, heart beating like a war drum.

There was no more waiting.

She had to find Dr. Elena Alvarez.

She had to act.

Before the whole world forgot.

5

Under Watchful Eyes

The night market pulsed like a hidden artery beneath the skin of the city—throbbing with movement, breath, and barely-contained desperation. Lanterns swung overhead, their recycled plastics glowing with bio-dyes that turned the streets into a surreal river of color. The flickering light danced on the cracked tiles and faces of the forgotten, illuminating everything and nothing at once.

Mira moved through the crowd with her hood drawn low and her satchel pressed tight to her side. She walked like a shadow— part of the chaos but never *in* it. Beneath her coat, her fingers curled protectively around the data drive nestled against her ribs. It pulsed like a second heartbeat, tiny and unassuming, yet heavy with the weight of truths that could unravel a nation.

The air was thick with scents that teased nostalgia—pepper, ginger, clove—and something almost like vanilla, though Mira suspected it came from synthetic aroma capsules, not any real pod. Still, it worked. Memory stirred, warmed, ached. She walked past stalls hawking bootleg antibiotics, repurposed solar slates, cracked cybernetic implants, and rehydrated fruit slices laid out like treasure under smeared plexi. Voices rose and fell in a babel of barter: offers, curses, laughter, longing.

A woman played a glass-string harp near a barricade of broken crates. Its eerie music made the air shimmer. Beside her, a barefoot child spun in slow circles, giggling beneath a rusting umbrella. Life, even here, had not surrendered.

Here, in this flickering underbelly of resistance and survival, anonymity had a heartbeat.

And Mira was counting on it.

She spotted Jonah near a vendor booth cluttered with salvaged electronics and counterfeit ID chips. He was hunched over a tray of circuit boards, soldering something with the calm focus of someone who had lived too long at the edge of danger. The blue-white torchlight flickered across his face, casting gold into the dark curls that fell into his eyes.

"Looking to upgrade?" he said without glancing up, his tone casual, playful—exactly what it needed to be.

"Depends," Mira murmured, stepping beside him. "Do you have anything that makes the truth louder?"

He stilled. Then looked up. His eyes met hers—deep brown, sharp, and tired in the way that only people who have *seen too much* can be.

"Mira," he breathed, her name catching like a lifeline on his tongue.

"Not here," she whispered. "Walk with me."

They melted into the crowd as if they'd always belonged, weaving through the press of bodies like smoke. Shoulder to shoulder, eyes forward. Mira reached into her pocket and withdrew a tightly folded scrap of parchment. She passed it to Jonah beneath the guise of examining a bruised fruit from a vendor's stall. Jonah unfolded it discreetly, his eyes scanning the clipped document: a declassified deployment schedule tied to the earliest clusters of memory loss. Just a sliver from the Vault—but it was enough.

"Where did you get this?" he asked, voice lower now.

"My father. He hid it. Professor Malik found me—said SkyShield wasn't just a climate fix. Said it started everything."

Jonah's brow furrowed. "This… this isn't just damning. It's radioactive."

"I know."

"And you're walking around with it like it's a shopping list?"

"I'm done being afraid," she said. "I need to find Dr. Elena Alvarez. She might have the missing pieces."

Jonah blew out a slow breath, his thumb brushing the edge of the document before slipping it into his jacket. "I always knew your dad didn't vanish by choice. They silenced him. He was asking too many questions. But I didn't know…"

His words trailed off.

A high-pitched hum pierced the night, cutting above the din like a scalpel. Mira's pulse jumped.

An AI surveillance orb coasted into view above the market—a sleek, disk-shaped drone with a scanning beam that rotated like a spotlight, sweeping over heads. Its lens pulsed, collecting biometric data, mapping the crowd like prey.

Mira stiffened. "Don't look up," she hissed.

Jonah didn't. Instead, he reached into his coat and palmed a black cylinder no bigger than a lighter. Its surface was scratched, wires protruding like nerves.

"I call it a ghost's umbrella," he muttered. "Watch."

He thumbed the switch.

The orb faltered.

Its beam flickered. Then jerked sideways, scanning in

stuttering arcs before veering off toward the harbor, confused by phantom signals.

"EMP disruptor," Jonah explained. "Crude but effective. Buys us thirty seconds. Maybe forty."

"That's enough," Mira said, her voice tight.

They ducked into a narrow corridor behind a noodle stand, steam curling around them like smoke from an old dream. They emerged into a dim alley lined with trash bins and cracked neon signs advertising things no one could afford anymore.

There, beneath the safe gloom, Mira finally exhaled.

"I can't do this alone," she said.

Jonah leaned against the wall, folding his arms. "Then it's good you found me."

"I'm scared, Jonah," she admitted, looking down. "Not for myself. For Lena. If something happens to me—if they get to me—she's all alone."

Jonah was quiet for a long moment. Then he said, "She won't be. I swear it. You're not the only one who remembers how to fight."

She looked up. And in his eyes, she saw what she needed: not just belief, but *faith*. Faith in her. Faith in *them*.

"Come on," he said. "I have a place. Off-grid. Ugly as hell, but no one will find us there."

They moved quickly through a labyrinth of forgotten backstreets—old maintenance routes and disused service tunnels, remnants of a city that had once sprawled without care. Mira followed as Jonah led her through rusted doors, down stairwells with graffiti warnings, past rooms where voices whispered stories in the dark.

Finally, he stopped at what looked like a solid wall.

He pried open a warped utility panel and ducked inside.

"Home sweet resistance," he said.

The room was small, lit by strung battery lamps and humming with repurposed tech. Cables slithered across the floor like living veins. Holoscreens blinked in standby, while old keyboards sat piled like bones. The walls were covered in overlapping maps, string charts, notes scribbled in marker and grease pencil. Some were diagrams. Others were poems.

Mira dropped her satchel and sat on the floor. She didn't speak for a minute. Just breathed.

Jonah sat beside her. "Tomorrow," he said, "we find the contact who knows where Alvarez went off-grid. It'll be dangerous. The Authority's watching everything. There's talk of a seditionist list."

"I'm probably at the top," Mira muttered.

"Then let's make it *worth* it," he said. "Let's give them a reason to be afraid."

He reached over and gently took her hand.

"I'm with you. All the way."

Mira looked at him—this hacker with sparks in his blood and fire in his spine—and for the first time in days, she felt the tightness in her chest ease.

"Thank you," she said.

"Don't thank me yet."

Outside, the city growled and blinked and stared with electronic eyes.

But inside, in this quiet heartbeat beneath its skin, something had awakened.

Not just truth.

Not just resistance.

But a spark.

A *promise*.

Tomorrow, they would move.
But tonight—they remembered.
And they were not alone.

6

The Lost Scientist

The farther they moved from the trembling core of New Harbor, the more the city began to dissolve into something half-forgotten. Propaganda posters tore in the wind, their curled edges peeling like sunburnt skin, slogans half-faded: *UNITY IS MEMORY, OBEDIENCE IS PEACE.* They clung to walls with no strength left to lie. Streetlights blinked erratically or not at all. Entire intersections had crumbled into sinkholes, consumed by creeping moss and the slow, patient hunger of nature reclaiming what humanity had failed to preserve. Surveillance drones no longer patrolled these zones— their routes abandoned, their AI systems rerouted to higher-threat districts. Only rusted sentry towers remained, staring down at nothing with hollow eyes.

Here, the city had stopped pretending it was alive.

Beneath the roar of an elevated expressway long closed to public traffic, Mira and Jonah moved with measured purpose. Above them, the highway hummed like a ghost throat, vibrating with freight trucks that still supplied the Authority's upper-tier enclaves. Down here, in the concrete underworld, only memories traveled freely.

Their destination crouched in the shadows beneath the overpass like a scar. A makeshift clinic, cobbled together from salvaged shipping containers, cracked prefab panels, and military-issue canvas tarps. Rust-streaked floodlights buzzed faintly from portable solar packs. Hand-cranked lanterns added their weak glow, casting crooked shadows that made everything look like it was trembling.

The scent of the place hit Mira before anything else—damp wool, rubbing alcohol, mold, and the undercurrent of too many unwashed bodies pressed into too small a space. It was the smell of forgotten people surviving anyway.

Inside, the low murmurs of exhaustion barely rose above the occasional hacking cough or moan. Patients wandered like ghosts between the rows of cots. Some murmured to themselves in broken loops—repeating names, dates, street addresses. Others clutched stained notebooks or scribbled reminders on their own skin, only to forget they'd done so a moment later. A girl, no older than Lena, sat on the floor staring at her open palms like they were unfamiliar tools. A lullaby floated through the air—wordless, tuneless, sung by a woman rocking herself back and forth in the corner.

Mira swallowed hard. Her stomach clenched. The Forgetting wasn't just theory here. It was a tide, slow and inevitable, crashing silently over everything it touched.

"This is where she works," Jonah whispered beside her. His voice had changed—lower, more reverent. "She's the only reason this place is still running."

Mira's eyes scanned the clinic until they caught a figure moving with quiet authority near the far end. A woman in a stained lab coat moved between cots with the speed of someone who'd had to make every second count for years. Her dark hair was streaked with iron-gray, pulled back into a utilitarian knot. Her face was lined, not just with age but purpose.

Dr. Elena Alvarez.

Jonah stepped forward first. "Dr. Alvarez?"

The woman froze mid-step.

Her eyes snapped to him. "No names," she hissed, voice sharp as wire. "Not here. Leave. Now."

Mira stepped in front of him, urgency rising like heat. "Please—just look at this."

From her satchel, she withdrew one of the Vault documents, carefully unfolded despite its brittleness. She held it like a peace offering. Alvarez's name was printed across the top beneath Carlo Solis's signature.

The doctor's face paled.

"I found this in my father's vault," Mira said, voice steady. "He was Carlo Solis. I'm his daughter."

Alvarez took the paper with trembling hands. Her eyes flicked across the text. Her shoulders slumped.

"I thought... you looked familiar," she murmured, almost to herself. "You have his eyes."

Mira's throat tightened. "He trusted you."

Alvarez nodded once. Then motioned toward a curtain near the back. "Come. Quickly."

They slipped behind the hanging sheet into a smaller room—barebones, lit only by the flicker of a cracked screen and a dented lantern strung from a rusting ceiling beam. The table was covered in handwritten notes, a half-eaten protein bar, and what looked like a neural scanner built from scavenged components.

Alvarez pulled the curtain shut and turned, her face stripped of resistance now—just tired honesty. "How much do you know?"

"Not enough," Mira admitted. "He knew SkyShield was dangerous. That it was tied to the Forgetting. He tried to stop it. You were there. You *know*."

Alvarez rubbed her forehead. "I was part of the team that engineered SkyShield. At first, we believed in it—a real solution to the runaway heat index. But when the memory disruption reports came in from test zones, we realized something was wrong. People were forgetting routines. Family names. Then whole weeks."

She pulled a photo from a nearby drawer—a faded, dog-eared image. Four scientists smiling, half-drunk on hope. Mira's father stood beside Alvarez, holding a notebook like it was scripture. They looked like people who thought they were saving the world.

"Celeste Drake was our director," Alvarez said darkly. "When we brought her the data, she said revealing it would collapse the project. 'Sacrifice the many to save the planet,' she said. We argued. Carlo documented everything. She silenced half our team. Others just… vanished."

"Why didn't you stop her?" Mira asked, her voice cracking.

"I tried," Alvarez said, guilt thick in her tone. "But your father did more. He risked everything. When I realized how far it would go—what they'd do—I disappeared. Came here. Been trying to atone ever since."

Mira blinked back tears. "He died thinking no one believed him."

Alvarez stepped forward and took Mira's hand. "He didn't die in vain. He left you the truth. And now, you brought it back to me. That matters."

Before Mira could speak, the air split with sound—a voice over a megaphone: "This facility is under inspection. By order of the Authority, stand down and prepare for identity verification."

Jonah cursed, his hand flying to the pistol beneath his coat.

"They found us," Alvarez whispered. "How?"

"They tracked me," Mira said, ice in her chest. "From the archive. From Malik. I led them here."

"No blame now," Jonah snapped, already yanking a supply crate from the floor to reveal a trapdoor. "Out. Now."

Boots pounded the ground outside. The flap of the clinic's main tent was ripped open. Shouts. Gunfire cracked. Patients screamed.

Just as Mira dropped into the hatch, a confused patient wandered into the path of an approaching guard. The enforcer paused. The patient blinked at him. "Am I... supposed to be here?" he asked, voice trembling.

It bought them four precious seconds.

They crawled beneath the floorboards, down a narrow tunnel. The smell was foul—mud, rust, blood. Jonah took the lead, flashlight between his teeth, one hand clutching Alvarez's. Mira brought up the rear, heart hammering.

Above, the enforcers tore through the clinic. Screams echoed. The lullaby faltered.

"We need to go deeper," Alvarez gasped. "Follow me."

She led them out through a crack in the foundation, past a collapsed stairwell, into an alley that stank of stagnant rain. From there, through another alley, past a burned-out storefront, to the skeleton of an old newsstand. Behind it: a drainage tunnel, nearly invisible under the debris.

They dropped inside, soaked and gasping.

Flashlights combed the sky above them. But down here...
silence.

They followed the tunnel into the bowels of the city, dripping
and blind.

Finally, they reached it—an old subway platform, lost to
memory and maps. Jonah flipped on a generator. Weak light
bloomed across rusted tracks, scattered cots, half-eaten food
packs. A resistance hideout. Not much—but safe.

Jonah collapsed onto a bench, breathless. "Welcome to my
second-favorite hole in the ground."

Mira sank beside him, soaked and shivering. Her eyes turned
to Alvarez.

"Will you help us?" she asked, voice small.

The doctor nodded, her jaw set. "I should've done more. I'll
do it now."

For the first time, Mira felt something close to relief.

Not victory.

But a step closer.

Above them, the city kept forgetting.

Below, truth sharpened its edges.

And the fight was far from over.

7

Revelations in the Dark

The storm still whispered above them, a gentle, ceaseless hush of rainfall threading through cracked concrete and rusted pipes, like the broken lullaby of a city too exhausted to scream. Inside Jonah's hidden lair, the hum of scavenged tech and the flicker of flickering LED strips cast dancing shadows across the walls—walls papered in maps, wiring diagrams, access schematics, and hand-scrawled notes that looked equal parts revolutionary and elegiac.

It was more than a hideout. It was a memory chamber. A bunker for belief.

Mira sat cross-legged on the cold concrete floor, the Vault's files spread before her like sacred relics. Faded documents, sealed data drives, yellowing blueprints—they formed a chaotic constellation of truth that had waited too long to be seen. She was tracing a path, not just across coordinates, but across the hushed betrayals of the past.

Beside her, Dr. Elena Alvarez leaned close, cracked glasses perched on the bridge of her nose, the shadows of her years drawn across her face like delicate ink. Her fingers trembled slightly as she pointed to a series of red-marked points on a SkyShield deployment schematic.

"This one," she murmured, tapping the sheet. "Coastal Spain. 2035. First cluster of reported memory degradation. The aerosol had only just been released into the upper atmosphere. No one expected the fallout to… land."

Jonah stood nearby, arms folded, silhouetted against a wall of flickering monitors displaying static and flickering news feeds. "How did it spread so fast?"

Alvarez's voice darkened. "It didn't just linger in the atmosphere. It rained. It settled into reservoirs, soaked into soil. It clung to plants and fish and the very air. It leeched into supply chains and water cycles. A whisper of unmaking, quiet and cruel. Not immediate, not loud. Just… gradual disappearance."

Mira's gaze drifted to a brittle photograph clipped to a file— her father, Dr. Carlo Solis, half-smiling beside a data console, his eyes full of urgency even then.

"And she knew," Mira said, her voice quiet but flint-hard. "Celeste Drake knew."

Alvarez nodded slowly. "I showed her the risk projections myself. Sixty percent degradation over ten years in all exposed civilian populations. More in the coastal and agricultural zones. She looked me in the eye and said, 'We'll lose more to fear than to forgetting.' She thought ignorance was stability."

Jonah shook his head, bitter. "And the antidote? There *was* one, wasn't there?"

Alvarez hesitated. Then sighed. "Yes. We tried to halt the compound's effects. In lab conditions, we developed a treatment that slowed or reversed the damage—if caught early enough. But before we could refine it, before we could offer it to the public, the directive came down: 'Classify all trials.

Secure formula. Terminate project.' They locked it up."

"Did anyone get it?" Mira asked, already knowing the answer.

"The elite," Alvarez said grimly. "The top-tier officials. Celeste. Her cabinet. Their families. They were inoculated before full deployment."

The words landed like shrapnel.

Mira's thoughts reeled, flashing back to Lena staring blankly at their kitchen table, to her father forgetting her name, to the long line of patients wandering the makeshift clinic. A world unraveling from the inside out while the ones who caused it watched from behind their immunity.

She clenched her fists. "They erased us to save themselves."

"We remember," Jonah said, kneeling beside her. "And now, we make sure the world does too."

Mira looked down at the files, at the blurry photos and blacked-out transcripts, and shook her head. "This isn't enough. It's words. Paper. Proof, yes, but not what the world needs to *believe*. If we want people to see—really see—we need the physical evidence. The formula. A sample of the compound. A cure."

Jonah's eyes sharpened. "The Ministry of Science. Everything's stored beneath their Civic Dome. It's their central hub. If there's a vault for the cure, it's there."

Alvarez's expression turned grave. "You're talking about one of the most secure facilities on the continent. Retinal scans. Voiceprint gates. Heat-mapping drones. I helped write their security protocols. It was impenetrable then—and it's worse now."

"But you know the design," Mira pressed. "You know the layout. Where they'd hide the evidence."

"I know *enough*," Alvarez said. "It'll be dangerous. Almost suicidal."

"But it's the only way," Mira finished.

The plan formed between them like a spark catching dry leaves. Alvarez began sketching maps from memory, marking tunnels, intake vents, emergency exits. Jonah explained how he could deploy a temporary signal mask to confuse the dome's perimeter sensors. He even had a device capable of mimicking an official's clearance signal—for about ten seconds. Long enough, maybe, if everything went right.

Nothing ever went right.

They worked in silence broken only by the rustle of paper, the tap of pen against plastic, and the sighs of long-held fear being given shape.

But somewhere in the haze of plans and ink, Mira stepped back from the maps and pulled out her burner phone. A tiny, flickering signal.

One ring. Two. Then a voice, frail and laced with static.

"Mira?"

Mira's breath caught. "Hey, baby bird. I'm here."

There was a pause on the other end. "Where… where's *here?*"

Mira's throat tightened. "I'm sorry. I couldn't come back last night. But I'm okay. I promise."

"I woke up and I didn't know where you were," Lena said softly. "I forgot. I thought… maybe I forgot *you.*"

The words hit like a blade. Mira squeezed her eyes shut. "You'll never forget me. I won't let that happen. I'm going to fix this. I'm going to fix *everything.*"

"I don't want to be like Dad," Lena whispered. "I don't want to disappear."

Mira bit down hard on her knuckle, holding back the sob. "You won't," she choked out. "Not if I have anything to say about it."

When the call ended, Mira didn't move. Her face was wet. Her chest burned. She curled inward, silently shaking.

Jonah came to her without a word and wrapped a blanket around her shoulders. He sat beside her, his silence speaking louder than comfort.

Minutes passed before Alvarez knelt down in front of her. "Sometimes saving the world means losing pieces of it along the way," she said gently. "We don't do it because it's easy. We do it because someone has to."

Mira looked up.

"I can't let her slip away," she whispered. "Not like my dad did."

"You won't," Jonah said. "Not if we finish this."

Mira nodded. Slowly. She reached out. Took Jonah's hand. Then Alvarez's.

The three of them sat together, hands joined across papers stained with dust and truth and memory. The candlelight flickered around them like a heartbeat.

Tomorrow, they would walk into the lion's den.

Tonight, they remembered why they had to.

For Carlo Solis. For Lena. For every name erased by silence. This was no longer just resistance.

It was remembrance.

8

Into the Lion's Den

The Ministry of Science loomed ahead like a wound stitched shut with glass and steel, its polished façade gleaming dully beneath the smothered sky. No moonlight dared touch it. No birds ever landed on its angular ridges. It stood apart from the ruins around it—untouched, unsullied, inhuman. Mira stared up at it from behind her respirator, the chill in her chest as biting as the night air. She felt small and heavy all at once, her identity stitched together by lies, hope, and a stolen clearance badge.

Beside her, Jonah adjusted the collar of his ill-fitting lab coat, his expression taut with focus. On his chest, the fake ID tag shimmered faintly with an embedded light sequence that mimicked bio-authentication. Dr. Elena Alvarez stood tall between them, her eyes fixed on the building she once helped design. She looked like a woman standing on the edge of a grave—half penance, half fury.

"You remember the layout?" Jonah murmured, barely moving his lips.

"I remember everything they wanted me to forget," Alvarez

said quietly. "Including where the monsters sleep."

Their forged credentials had passed muster at the outer fence—a perimeter patrolled by drones and bored guards with stunners slung casually over one shoulder. The guards had barely glanced at the ident chips Jonah flashed from his tablet. The Authority's overconfidence was its greatest weakness. So far, Alvarez's knowledge of outdated security protocols and the emergency clearance code gifted by a resistance mole had carried them through the lobby and two internal checkpoints.

But every step deeper into the building's glacial heart felt like sinking into the belly of a beast—a beast that catalogued every heartbeat and didn't forget the taste of traitors.

Inside, the Ministry was pristine and sterile. White walls gleamed with surgical coldness, and every surface reflected light in ways that made it hard to tell if you were looking at yourself or the version of you the system wanted to see. The air smelled of bleach and hidden sins.

They moved with slow confidence, mimicking the pace of the few researchers they passed. Masks and gloves obscured most faces, and no one made eye contact. Here, invisibility wasn't stealth—it was policy. They passed corridors of glass-walled laboratories where figures in hazmat suits moved like ghosts, tending to experiments behind sealed doors. No conversation. No music. Just machines humming softly like they were dreaming.

The retinal scanner outside the restricted wing pulsed red. Mira held her breath. Alvarez stepped forward.

"Override code 19-Gamma," she said.

There was a pause that stretched like a noose tightening.

Then the scanner blinked green.

The door hissed open.

And the nightmare stepped into the light.

The corridor beyond was clinical—yes—but also monstrous. Glass cases lined the walls, each one containing a tragic scene in miniature. Lab rats with electrodes stitched to their skulls, running endlessly in circles. Holo-monitors cycling through brain scans covered in red zones, the labels reading "Degeneration Stage 3," "Cortical Disintegration," "Terminal."

A screen flickered with the image of a young girl—no older than Lena—mouthing her name in repetition: "Lia. Lia. Lia…" until her voice cracked and she screamed instead.

Mira's stomach twisted. The bile rose in her throat like betrayal. This wasn't science. This was ritualized erasure.

"They never stopped testing," Alvarez said bitterly. "Even after the data was buried. This is their hidden temple. They worship control."

A junction loomed ahead. Fluorescent light buzzed above, sickly and white.

"This is it," Alvarez said, pausing. "Server room's to the right. Jonah—"

"I've got it," he said. "I'll pull every file tagged with SkyShield, Forgetting, antidote trials, Celeste Drake. Meet you in the vault."

Mira caught his arm before he went. "Be safe."

He gave her a crooked smile. "That's not the goal. Survive. That's the goal."

Then he was gone, disappearing into the shadows like a whisper.

Mira and Alvarez continued down the corridor, past labs and climate-controlled vaults. The deeper they went, the colder it became—an engineered chill designed to preserve specimens and discourage loitering. The silence pressed in, too dense to breathe.

At last, they reached the biostorage chamber—a door labeled: BIO-SECURE: LEVEL 5 CLEARANCE REQUIRED.

Alvarez's hand hesitated over the keypad.

"Last time I was here," she whispered, "they asked me to destroy the formula."

"Did you?"

"No," she said. "I lied."

The door slid open.

Inside, the room shimmered with sub-zero containment. Frost glazed the cabinets, and the hum of coolant units droned like distant thunder. Every step left a print in the condensation-covered floor.

Alvarez moved to one of the drawers and keyed in a sequence. With a hiss of released pressure, the drawer slid out.

Inside: glass vials with silver-blue liquid. Labels printed in tiny text: SKYSHIELD COMPOUND – BATCH 17A.

Mira's fingers hovered above them. "This is it?"

"The poison," Alvarez said. "The first generation of the aerosol compound. It's… what started it all."

Mira slipped three vials into a padded case and tucked them into her satchel. They rattled faintly, like guilt in a box.

Another drawer. This one marked: PROTOTYPE COUN-TERAGENTS – INTERNAL USE ONLY.

Alvarez opened it with both hands.

Syringes. Dozens. Each marked with color-coded tabs. She stared for a moment, then reached in.

"We called it MN-Delta," she said. "It wasn't perfect. But it worked. The Authority suppressed it before the public ever heard its name."

Her fingers closed around five vials and a data chip of formula sequencing. "We can replicate it. If we live long enough."

Then the lights turned red.

A shrieking alarm split the air.

"INTRUSION DETECTED. LEVEL 3 CONTAINMENT LOCK INITIATED."

Mira's blood froze.

"Jonah," she gasped. "He triggered something."

They ran.

Doors hissed closed behind them as lockdown protocols engaged. Shutters slammed down with brutal finality. Security barriers lit up in crimson arcs.

They rounded a corner just as a blast door descended—but not fast enough.

They slid under.

Ahead, they saw the server room door propped open. Jonah knelt at the terminal, typing furiously. Data flickered across the screen—emails, schematics, risk reports, internal memos with Celeste Drake's name in bold.

"Hurry!" Mira shouted.

"Almost—!" he panted. "Ninety-seven percent. Ninety-nine— got it!"

He yanked the drive free.

Boots thundered behind them. Gunfire rang out in the upper corridors. Mira turned toward the hall they'd entercd —sealed. No escape.

Then her eyes landed on a wall panel beside a sealed ventilation grate.

A red switch. Emergency Purge.

Mira grabbed Alvarez's sleeve. "Will it open that grate?"

Alvarez nodded. "For sixty seconds. Then it seals again."

Mira hit the switch.

A deafening roar of suction burst through the corridor. The panel beside the grate unlocked and swung open.

Jonah clutched the drive. Alvarez the cooler. Mira grabbed both and dove.

They plunged into a maintenance shaft lined with frost and echo. Rungs clattered beneath them as they descended. Above, flashlights cut through smoke and noise.

Then silence.

Just the sound of their breath.

And the knowledge that they were no longer just seekers.

They were thieves of truth, clutching the cure like fire in their hands.

They had the evidence.

Now, they had to survive it.

9

Fire and Flight

The Ministry's innards roared with alarm. Red lights pulsed like blood through arteries of steel and wire. Sirens wailed in rounds, echoing off metallic walls with a panic that grew louder with every breath. Mira sprinted through the narrowing corridors, the soles of her boots slapping hard against grated steel. Her lungs heaved. Her heart galloped. Her satchel—stuffed with the vials, the data drive, the fragile cargo of truth—beat against her hip like a warning bell.

Behind her, Jonah kept pace, the drive clutched to his chest as if it were his own heart. Dr. Elena Alvarez ran beside them, clutching the cooler under her arm. Despite her age and the lab coat flapping behind her like a ghost's shroud, she moved with purpose.

But Mira could see it now—etched into the corners of Elena's eyes, tightening the muscles in her jaw.

Not just fear.

Not just focus.

Resolution. As if she already knew how this would end.

"We turn left here!" Elena barked, breath hitching. "Service tunnels loop to the sub-loading dock. If we make it—"

"We *will*," Mira snapped.

They veered into a narrower corridor, the walls coated in dripping condensation. Pipes hissed steam at intervals like mechanical serpents. Warning panels blinked orange and red, the systems confused by overlapping emergencies.

Somewhere above, a voice barked through the loudspeakers:

"Level three breach. Unauthorized personnel detected. Lethal force authorized."

Jonah winced. "They're not playing around."

"Then neither are we," Mira said through gritted teeth.

Behind them, the screech of drones grew sharper. Buzzing, darting, scanning.

The corridor twisted into a maintenance catwalk strung above a lower floor of exposed ductwork. They vaulted it in turns, boots thudding, hands catching on rails that trembled with age. Mira landed hard on the far side and turned to help Alvarez down.

They pushed forward—breathless, hunted, burning.

And then they passed it.

A side observation chamber. Walls of reinforced glass.

Mira caught it out of the corner of her eye and skidded to a halt.

"No…"

Inside, rows of patients lay on medical slabs, heads bandaged, tubes snaking from IVs to their spines. Electrodes blinked across their foreheads. Some were crying. Some simply stared. One woman mouthed a word Mira couldn't hear—over and over again. Her fingers trembled against the straps that held her down.

Jonah froze beside her. "They're still running trials. Even

after everything."

Elena looked like she might shatter. "This wasn't part of the mandate. It wasn't... This was supposed to be treatment. Not this. Never this."

"They're experimenting on them," Mira whispered, numb. "They're *studying* the disease they caused."

A flicker of movement in the glass.

One of the patients—a teenage boy—turned his head and looked right at her. He didn't know her. Might never know his own name again.

But his eyes begged: Remember me.

Mira tore herself away.

No more detours. No more horror.

This had to end.

They pushed onward.

The corridor narrowed again, curving toward the loading bay exit. The last chance.

Mira's hope flickered. Maybe—maybe they'd made it.

But then she saw it.

The blast door.

Sealed. Heavy. Cold.

A red status light blinked, mocking them.

"No," she whispered.

Elena lunged for the keypad, typing furiously. Mira slammed her hand against the emergency override. Nothing. The screen remained blank.

"No power reroute," Elena said. "They've locked it down remotely."

Behind them, the sound of pursuit closed in. Orders shouted. Boots clattered. Mira's breath hitched in her throat.

"This can't be it," Jonah said, backing up. "There has to be another way."

"There isn't," Elena said.

She turned slowly, meeting Mira's eyes. The weight of years fell into that gaze—years of silence, guilt, failure. She reached into her coat and pressed the antidote pouch into Mira's hands.

"You're the one who makes it out."

"No," Mira said, voice cracking. "No, we're all going."

"You don't understand," Elena said, her voice low and unwavering. "I walked away once. Let others bear the burden. I won't do it again."

"We can find another way—"

"Mira," she said gently, firmly. "Carlo gave everything for the truth. I won't be the one who lets it die in this hallway."

Before Mira could speak again, Elena stepped into the center of the corridor.

A spotlight snapped on. Drones zipped into view. Guards rounded the bend, guns up.

"I'm Dr. Elena Alvarez!" she shouted, hands raised. "I acted alone. No one else was involved."

"No!" Mira surged forward—but Jonah caught her around the waist, pulling her into the shadows of a maintenance duct half-hidden in the wall.

"Let me go!" she sobbed, struggling.

"She *wants* you to run!" Jonah hissed. "Don't waste what she just gave us!"

Through the grate, Mira watched the impossible unfold.

The guards encircled Elena. She didn't fight. Didn't speak again. But her eyes found Mira's through the shadows.

One last nod.

One final, defiant smile.

Then they dragged her away.

And she was gone.

The scream inside Mira didn't leave her lips. It settled in her chest like ash.

"She saved us," she whispered, her throat raw.

"I know," Jonah said softly. "And we'll make sure it wasn't for nothing."

They moved through the duct in silence. It twisted downward, deeper, older—into forgotten sub-basements and boiler passages no longer on Ministry maps.

At last, they emerged behind the facility. Steam hissed from ruptured pipes. The industrial district beyond lay half-drowned in toxic runoff and shadow.

Sirens continued to scream, but the night no longer chased them. The hunt had moved on.

For now.

They crouched beneath an overhang as the sky began to shift—dark blue giving way to crimson.

Dawn.

Except it wasn't gold. Not clean. The sun fought its way through a veil of artificial particles—SkyShield's legacy.

The light was wrong.

Beautiful in a broken kind of way.

Mira stared at it, hands shaking.

In her satchel: three vials of poison, five doses of the cure, and a data drive full of secrets that could burn the world clean.

She turned to Jonah.

"We finish this," she said.

He nodded.

And together, they vanished into the morning haze—fire trailing behind them.

10

Truth on the Brink

The church was crumbling.

Time had not been kind to the bones of St. Aurelia's. Its spires had collapsed long ago, eaten by storms and salt, its pews stripped for firewood in the first blackout winter. Ivy had breached the walls like an invading army, curling through shattered stained glass and painting the stone floor in fractured, prismatic wounds. Sunlight poured through the half-collapsed roof in long, sacred shafts—but it brought no warmth, only the ghostly silence of abandonment.

Beneath the hollow shell of the altar, Mira and Jonah lay hidden in the shadows, hearts racing, backs pressed against cold stone, the weight of a nation's buried sins crammed into a single weathered satchel between them.

Mira's shoulder throbbed where the metal rungs of the Ministry's purge shaft had scraped skin from bone. Jonah's brow was crusted with dried blood from where a pipe had kissed him too hard during their escape. They had no medical kits, no ointments, no comfort—just an old wool scarf Mira had torn in silence and wrapped around Jonah's head with trembling fingers. Her hands had bled onto the fabric. Neither of them mentioned it.

They hadn't spoken in hours.

They listened instead—to the murmur of doves roosting in the rafters, the wind threading through the rafters like breath, and the distant, inescapable hum of the city slowly waking again to the lies it had been fed.

Then, overhead, a buzz split the air—precise, predatory.

A surveillance drone.

Mira and Jonah held still, their bodies flat against the stone floor, barely daring to breathe.

The drone slowed as it passed the arched opening above the altar. Its speaker crackled to life, casting an artificial calm over the broken nave.

"Urgent bulletin from the Unity Authority," it intoned. "Dr. Elena Alvarez has been arrested on charges of treason and subversive science fraud. In a statement from Minister Celeste Drake, the public is reminded that spreading falsehoods about the Forgetting is an act of sedition."

A projector flared, casting a distorted holo across the far wall. Amid peeling saints and war-stained murals, Celeste Drake's face emerged like a corrupted halo—perfectly lit, perfectly composed, eyes cold as winter marble.

Her voice rang through the ruins like a psalm of power.

"The rumors circulating about SkyShield are dangerous misinformation designed to destabilize our recovery. There is no conspiracy—only cowards who seek to profit from fear. We will find those responsible. And we will restore order."

The image blinked out.

The drone veered away.

And silence took its place.

Mira stared at the stone where Celeste's image had hovered, her eyes wide, unfocused, rage and sorrow mixing behind them like stormclouds.

"She's already rewriting it," she said hollowly. "Elena. My father. They're calling them traitors. Sick. Delusional."

Her voice cracked.

"They'll make the world forget them before it ever knows what they did."

She curled into herself, clutching her knees as if trying to keep herself from unraveling.

Jonah reached into the satchel and pulled out the drive, its steel case smudged with soot and blood. He opened his tablet and connected it. The glow of the screen lit up their faces like a tiny campfire, casting truth into the darkness.

File after file bloomed across the cracked glass.

Reports. Surveillance footage. Graphs. Memos. Password-protected folders now unlocked with Elena's codes.

A video file loaded—Celeste Drake in a secure briefing room, her voice sharp and clear:

"We cannot afford panic. If we release this data, we lose control. Limit internal access. The public only gets what we give them. We'll say it's environmental trauma, stress, post-crisis cognitive decline—anything but the compound."

Mira flinched.

Another video: a grainy feed from a restricted storage warehouse. Rows of boxes, each stamped: ANTIDOTE – EXECUTIVE DISTRIBUTION ONLY. Guards paced lazily. One laughed as he lit a cigarette. At the bottom of the feed, the date blinked: 7 **years ago**.

Jonah looked at her. "This isn't speculation. It's proof."

Mira nodded slowly. "If we show this… they can't ignore it.

The people will rise. They'll demand the cure. Demand *justice*."

"But how?" Jonah asked. "We can't leak this to the networks. They'll bury it. Track us. Kill it before it breathes."

Mira's brow furrowed. "There has to be a way."

"There is," Jonah said softly. "The Emergency Broadcast System. Built before the Unity Authority took power. It still runs on the old infrastructure—relay towers, satellites. It's analog. Ugly. But they can't censor it in real time."

Mira blinked. "A pirate signal?"

He nodded. "The biggest one in history."

They sat in silence for a long moment, the weight of what he'd said blooming like fire between them.

And then Mira reached into her coat and drew out something she'd barely dared to look at since the Ministry: a soft pouch containing five glass vials, glowing faintly blue.

The antidote.

Elena's last gift.

Mira cradled them in her hands like glass birds.

"I could use one," she whispered. "Give one to Lena. We could disappear. Quietly. Just... *live*. Hide. Forget the war."

She didn't look up.

"I could save her. Tonight."

Jonah didn't answer.

Then, gently, "Is that what you want?"

"I don't know," she choked. "I just— I'm so tired, Jonah. Of losing. I've lost my father. My mother. Elena. I don't want to lose my sister too."

She shook her head. Tears glimmered in her eyes.

"I'm so tired of sacrificing."

Jonah reached out and touched her hand.

"I know," he said quietly. "But this... this isn't just about you.

Or me. It's about every child whispering their own name in the dark. Every mother who can't remember her son's face. Every life they decided wasn't worth saving."

He leaned closer.

"If we do this… we don't just save Lena. We save *everyone's* Lena."

Mira stared at him, breath ragged.

And slowly… she nodded.

Resolve returned to her like breath after drowning.

"Then we broadcast," she said.

They moved quickly, purposefully.

Mira laid out the documents: maps, graphs, timelines. Jonah decrypted the most damaging files and compressed the footage. They created redundancies—multiple drives, multiple copies, printed proofs. Mira wrote a short statement by hand, to be read aloud in case the data feeds failed.

As the sky darkened outside, the church filled with a strange energy—a hum of rebellion born in ruins.

Mira stood before the altar where saints once watched the faithful, her eyes blazing in the candlelight.

"This is it," she said.

Jonah slung the satchel over his shoulder.

"This is our line in the sand."

Outside, night wrapped the city in shadows.

But inside that broken church, two fugitives sat among the ghosts—quiet, scarred, but not afraid.

Because they held the truth.

And tomorrow, they would burn the sky with it.

11

The Die Is Cast

Night had hollowed out the city.
Mira and Jonah moved like phantoms through its bones, weaving silently between sandbag barricades and razor-wire fences. The streets were bare, but pressure simmered beneath every surface—like a storm held in a clenched fist. Martial law had clamped down tight, sealing the city into silence. Overhead, curfew drones buzzed like mechanical wasps, their lenses glowing with predatory red light, barking the same message over and over in sterile voices:

"Return to shelter. Unauthorized movement after curfew will result in detainment and memory health screening. This is for your safety."

Every building they passed seemed to watch them, as if the walls themselves had learned to whisper. Government banners hung limp from skeletal lampposts, the Unity Authority's symbol—an unbroken circle—emblazoned in endless repetition. But even here, at the regime's core, the cracks had begun to show.

Mira stopped suddenly beside a boarded-up storefront. Its

facade had been turned into a shrine. Murals painted in vibrant colors, fading in the acidic rain. Faces of children, elders, parents—dozens of them. Beneath each face, a name and a memory:

Leila, 6 – forgot her own name.

Hassan, 32 – wandered into the flood zone.

Amira, 14 – forgot how to speak.

Below the portraits, people had left offerings: wilting flowers, broken watches, candle stubs, puzzle pieces, photographs curled by moisture. Memory tokens, anchored in hope.

It looked like a cemetery without bodies.

Mira reached out and traced the paint gently with her fingertips. She closed her eyes.

This is why we fight. Not just for Lena. For all of them.

Jonah touched her arm lightly. "Checkpoint. Two blocks ahead."

They ducked into shadow behind a crumbled stairwell, watching as a patrol unit marched into view. Black-armored guards with mirrored visors flanked a mobile scan station. Tethered drones hovered just above their shoulders like hawks, eyes sweeping for heat signatures and movement.

Mira pulled her hood lower and reached into her coat, fingers curling around a forged ID card. The name on it was **Saria Hemsley – Technical Ops**. The photo was grainy. The credentials barely passable.

She handed Jonah a matching clearance badge. "Don't say anything unless they ask. Let me talk."

"Copy that," he murmured, adjusting his posture to match hers: calm, confident, indifferent.

They stepped from the alley and approached the checkpoint.

"ID scan," barked a guard.

Mira handed over the card. The scanner blinked blue, then yellow. The guard narrowed his eyes.

"You're out late, Tech Hemsley," he said. "Protocol states all tower ops were locked down after 2100 hours."

"Emergency recalibration," she said smoothly. "A network relay at Tower 3 began cycling feedback loops. We were dispatched under code seven override. Encryption staff's with me."

The guard turned the card over, inspecting it. "This ring—" he pointed. "Not regulation."

Mira's hand instinctively curled toward her finger—the thin gold band there. Her mother's wedding ring. The only thing she'd kept after the flood. She hesitated.

"A memento," she said softly. "One of the last things my mother remembered before she drowned."

The guard stared. Mira's heart thudded painfully.

Without blinking, she slid the ring from her finger and held it out. "If it's a problem, take it."

He looked at her for a long time. Then he took the ring, slid it into his vest, and waved them through.

"You didn't come through here," he said.

Mira nodded once, throat tight. They passed silently through the checkpoint, never once looking back.

Only when they reached the service access tunnel behind the TeleComm Tower did Mira finally let out a breath.

"He kept it," she muttered bitterly.

Jonah didn't ask what the ring meant. He didn't have to.

The tower loomed ahead—glass and steel rising into the smog-choked night like a monument to surveillance itself. Spotlights swept the sky from its crown, casting brief beams across the rooftops like the gaze of a sleeping god.

At its base, they stopped.

"Server room's two levels up that shaft," Mira said, pointing. "You'll upload the broadcast files. I'll handle the satellite uplink from the roof control deck."

Jonah gave her a long look. "Once this starts, we can't turn back."

"I know," she said. "It's time."

He reached into his bag and pulled out a small handgun—old, matte black, heavy with intent.

He handed it to her.

Mira looked at it like it was a snake.

"I've never—"

"Just in case," Jonah said quietly. "Point and breathe. That's all."

She nodded, slid the gun into her coat, and turned toward the stairwell.

The climb was brutal—twenty-eight floors through a forgotten maintenance shaft, lungs burning with each step, thighs trembling with exhaustion. Mira's vision blurred more than once. Every breath echoed in the narrow space.

Then—halfway up—she froze.

The marker on the wall was faded. The number: smeared, unreadable.

Her mind blanked.

What floor am I on?

Her heart thudded in panic.

Is it happening?

Am I forgetting?

Her chest tightened. She braced against the wall. Cold sweat beaded her spine.

Then—quietly—she began to speak.

"Red spoon... blue sock... green frog... yellow star..."

The memory game.

Lena's voice in her mind. The kitchen table. A laughing six-year-old clapping her hands in rhythm.

The panic ebbed. Her breathing slowed. The fog receded.

Floor 21.

She climbed on.

At the top, the rooftop control room awaited—a circular chamber of glass and light, towering above the sleeping city. Banks of instruments blinked gently. The satellite uplink terminal glowed, waiting.

She placed the mobile transmitter on the hub and connected the drive.

Jonah's voice crackled in her earpiece.

"I'm in the mainframe. Upload initialized. You've got five minutes to route the satellite signal and override the scramblers."

Her fingers danced across the touchscreen. Graphs loaded. Files queued. Encryption protocols broke open like eggshells.

The progress bar crawled up: **22%... 34%... 49%...**

Then—the siren.

A shriek through the tower's audio system. Red lights began to spin.

"Security breach detected. All levels on lockdown."

Mira froze.

"Jonah?" she whispered.

"They found me," he said breathlessly. "Doesn't matter. Upload's at 72%. Keep going. *Finish it.*"

Mira ran to the security monitor panel.

On-screen: black-armored operatives flooding the stairwells. Tactical formations. Rifles raised.

And at their center—unmistakable—walked Minister Celeste Drake.

Her uniform immaculate. Her expression unreadable.

"She's here," Mira said aloud, a cold chill wrapping her spine.

She sprinted to the door and slammed the emergency lock.

Then—barricaded the room.

Consoles. Shelving units. Metal stools. Her hands flew in desperation.

She turned to the satellite feed. **93%.**

She pulled out the gun. Held it with both hands.

It felt wrong. Cold. Alive.

Her breath came fast and shallow.

Outside the glass windows, the city pulsed in silence—an ocean of rooftops and distant lights.

Below, thousands of families. Thousands of memories.

And the truth, inching closer to daylight.

Mira steadied herself. She stepped forward, placed herself between the door and the terminal.

95%.

Footsteps. Getting closer.

96%.

She thought of her father. Of Lena's frightened voice. Of Elena's last look before the guards took her away.

97%.

She braced herself.

The world was about to change.

And Mira Solis would make sure it remembered.

12

The Choice

The steel door exploded inward with a deafening clang. The shockwave knocked Mira off balance, her arm scraping against the console as the barricade she'd so carefully assembled splintered and flew apart. Smoke billowed into the control room, mingling with sparks from a damaged panel. Dust rained from the ceiling tiles like ash from a slow-burning fire.

Through the haze stepped Minister Celeste Drake— impossibly composed, her uniform pristine, her expression carved from marble. She moved like a storm behind glass, accompanied by two armored agents in black, their rifles trained forward.

Behind her, the red-streaked dawn broke across the horizon, bathing the tower in bloodlight. The city glittered beneath the skyline—broken but awake, its people unaware of what was unfolding above them. Sirens echoed from below, the tower groaning under its own weight.

Inside the control room, the air felt thick enough to choke.

Mira stood protectively in front of the console. On its

flickering interface, the transmitter upload continued, slow and steady:

75%...

Her pulse roared in her ears.

"Leave us," Celeste said coolly, never looking at her guards. Her voice didn't rise. It didn't need to. It was the kind of voice people obeyed because they feared what would happen if they didn't.

The agents hesitated. Then stepped back, exiting with mechanical precision.

The door sealed behind them with a metallic *clang*, leaving only two women in the high chamber of glass and steel—the would-be tyrant and the would-be rebel.

For a long moment, neither moved. The tower hummed around them like a tuning fork, wires alive with tension.

"Mira Solis," Celeste said at last. "You've made quite the mess."

"I'm cleaning one up," Mira replied, steady.

Celeste's eyes swept the room. She took in the console, the upload status, the flickering relay. She walked slowly—unhurried, graceful, dangerous. The authority of decades radiated from her every movement.

"I remember your father, you know," she said, her voice smooth as honey. "He was brilliant. Passionate. A man who saw what was coming long before anyone else. He just didn't know what to do with that knowledge."

"Don't speak his name," Mira growled, her fists clenched.

"But I respected him," Celeste continued. "He was loyal. Until the end. He thought the public deserved the truth. But truth, Mira, is a weapon. It cuts in every direction. He didn't understand scale. He didn't see the chaos waiting behind transparency."

"No," Mira said. "He just believed people had the right to remember their own lives."

Celeste's gaze hardened. "And what would you have done, child? Watched the world burn? Watched nations collapse under the weight of fear and famine?"

"They're still collapsing," Mira spat. "But now they're doing it quietly. People fading in their beds, forgetting who they are. Families crumbling because of secrets. That's your world. That's your victory."

Celeste stepped closer. The console's glow painted the sharp lines of her face. "Do you know what it means to carry billions on your back? I made a choice that saved civilization from drowning. Yes—SkyShield had consequences. We didn't know the full scope."

"You *did*," Mira snapped. "You buried the data. You hoarded the cure."

"We had no cure," Celeste hissed, her calm beginning to crack. "We had *prototypes*. A fraction of what was needed. We did what was *necessary* to keep order while the world stabilized."

"You chose who mattered," Mira said. "You let people like Lena suffer so you could hold the reins. You let my father die ashamed. You made everyone forget to keep your grip on power."

Celeste went quiet.

Then she reached into her coat pocket—not for a weapon, but for a thin black tablet.

It blinked awake.

Mira's breath hitched.

Onscreen: a surveillance feed of a small holding cell. Inside it, Lena sat on the floor, knees tucked to her chest, arms wrapped around a ratty blanket. Her hair was damp. Her eyes were wide and glazed with fear.

"Lena," Mira whispered.

"She's safe," Celeste said. "For now. We retrieved her this morning—emergency medical transport. Your neighbors were concerned. Thought she'd been left alone too long."

"You took her," Mira said, voice hollow. "You *used* her."

"She's showing early signs of cognitive disruption. Likely stage one. But still treatable."

Mira's entire body went still.

"Let me guess," she said. "You'll treat her. If I give up."

Celeste nodded slowly. "Abort the transmission. Surrender the files. I'll cure your sister. No trial. No pursuit. You walk away. Both of you. You start over. No more fighting. No more fear."

Mira looked at the screen again. Lena blinked up at the ceiling, mouthing something Mira couldn't hear.

The console beeped behind her. The upload crept forward.

82%.

"And if I refuse?" Mira asked, barely audible.

Celeste's tone shifted—steel now. "Then she becomes a statistic. One of thousands. You know what happens to untreated cases. Memory loss. Dissociation. Neurological failure."

"You'd threaten a child?"

"I'm not threatening," Celeste said. "I'm *offering*. Mercy. A chance to live."

"You're threatening," Mira snapped. "With a gun pointed at her future."

Celeste raised her chin. "Don't test me."

The ultimatum hung in the air like the scent of fire.

Mira's hand hovered over the abort switch. Her heart

pounded.

One choice. Save her, or save them all.

The weight of it was unbearable.

Her mind reeled. *She could end this. Walk away. Disappear. No more danger. Just Lena. Alive.*

Then—her fingers found the edge of the pistol Jonah had given her.

She didn't draw it. Just felt its shape.

Her father's voice echoed in her memory, brittle and distant.

"Even if I forget… you must remember, mija. Hold on to the truth. Even when it hurts. *Especially* then."

Her chest seized. She took a breath. Her eyes burned.

I'm sorry, Lena.

She looked up.

Celeste's finger was on her tablet, ready to signal a medical override.

Mira met her gaze, shoulders squared.

"You've stolen memories," she said. "But you don't get to steal this choice."

Celeste didn't blink.

Mira stepped forward.

"I'm not your pawn. I won't trade the truth for comfort. Lena deserves more than a favor from a tyrant. She deserves a world that remembers."

The upload ticked upward—**90%… 91%…**

Celeste's face broke—just slightly. Her mask slipped. Her mouth tightened. Her eyes flared—not with fury alone, but with grief. Remorse. Rage.

She drew a sidearm.

"So be it," she whispered.

The barrel gleamed.

69

Mira didn't flinch.

She stepped into the path of the gun, shielding the console with her body.

The truth pulsed behind her.

Ready to rise.

Ready to burn.

13

The Light of Truth

The first gunshot cracked like thunder.

Mira dove to the floor. Pain lanced across her upper arm as the bullet grazed her, scorching a hot, ragged line through flesh and fabric. She hit the metal deck hard, her ribs jarring against the floor. For a second, everything blurred— sound, light, the very air spinning as stars bloomed behind her eyes. But even as she gasped, her hands moved instinctively, scrambling to shield the transmitter console, the beating heart of everything they'd fought for.

Celeste Drake's second shot blasted apart a monitor just inches from Mira's face. Sparks rained like angry fireflies. The console blinked wildly, but the progress bar kept climbing.

96%...

"MIRA!" Jonah's voice rang out from somewhere beyond the smoke and gunfire, ragged and desperate.

Then chaos surged.

The two armored agents flanked Celeste with military precision, bursting forward like unleashed wolves. One lunged for Mira. She screamed and swung wildly, the butt of Jonah's pistol connecting with a crunch against the agent's jaw. He stumbled—but the second grabbed her from behind, yanking her off her feet, pinning her arms.

She kicked. Twisted. Bit. There was no finesse, no plan—only raw, animal defiance. Her knee slammed into armor, her fingernails raked skin.

"You can't stop this!" she shouted through gritted teeth as she thrashed. "You're too late!"

The console flashed: **98%...**

Celeste shoved past the tangle of limbs and bodies, her expression warped with fury. She slammed her hand onto the console, stabbing at the abort command.

The screen blinked.

OVERRIDE LOCK ENGAGED. PASSWORD RE-QUIRED.

A shrill tone echoed from the speakers.

Celeste froze.

Mira, pinned and panting, looked up at her, blood on her lip and sweat dripping from her brow. Despite everything—despite pain and fear—she grinned through clenched teeth.

"Checkmate."

Jonah had anticipated this. Days ago, he and Mira had planned for the moment when brute force would try to end what truth had begun. The failsafe—a hardcoded lockdown protocol—could only be overridden with a two-key passphrase neither of them had written down.

Celeste's fury erupted like wildfire.

She dove for the transmitter cables, trying to rip them free. Her hands shook, her mouth snarling words Mira couldn't hear. She was unraveling. Cornered.

Then the door burst open again with a metallic shriek.

Jonah crashed into the room like a storm, blood streaked across his temple, one eye swollen shut. He was panting, wounded—but on fire. Without hesitation, he threw himself at the second agent, tackling him off Mira and sending them both tumbling into a desk with a sickening crash.

Mira rolled away, coughing, gasping for air.

"Jonah—!" she tried to rise, but her limbs trembled from adrenaline and blood loss.

Celeste shrieked, yanking on the last intact cord of the transmitter.

"No!"

Mira lunged. Their bodies collided with brutal force. She grabbed Celeste's wrist, twisting it. The cord slipped from her grasp. The pistol clattered across the floor.

They grappled, woman against woman, fists and elbows landing like hammers. Celeste slammed her fist into Mira's ribs. Mira struck back, elbow to throat. Blood smeared across the floor. Glass crunched beneath their boots.

Celeste kicked hard—Mira flew back, slamming into the edge of a console.

Before she could move, Celeste closed in, eyes blazing. She grabbed Mira by the collar, yanked her upright, and jammed a sidearm against her temple.

Everything stopped.

Even Jonah froze mid-fight, mid-breath. The room rang with alarms, blinking lights, blood, and static.

"You will shut it off," Celeste hissed, voice trembling with rage. "Or I swear—*you and your sister die right here.*"

Mira gasped, vision swimming, the cold barrel pressed against her skin like ice. Her body screamed to comply.

But then—she saw it.

Behind Celeste's shoulder, just on the console monitor:
99%...
And a small red icon Mira hadn't noticed before.
LIVE TRANSMISSION IN PROGRESS
Her breath hitched.
Jonah had done it.
The mic was hot.
Every word Celeste had spoken, every threat, every lie, was out there—flooding the networks. Carried by the ancient Emergency Broadcast System to every screen, every device, every radio tower. Across cities, across borders.
The truth was already out.
And Mira's voice—shaky, wounded, defiant—cut through the signal like a blade.
"You won't have that power for long."
100%
Transmission: LIVE.
Across the city, every screen turned black, then blazed to life with the first files: Dr. Solis's reports, redacted memos, SkyShield data overlays, timelines, casualty projections. Hidden footage played—celestial briefings, neurological charts, patients forgotten in cages.
Then Mira's voice echoed, everywhere.
"My name is Mira Solis. The Unity Authority is lying to you. The Forgetting wasn't an accident. It was a choice. Made by those who were supposed to protect us."
In a thousand homes, hands covered mouths.
In clinics, nurses dropped syringes. In shelters, people wept.
In the Ministry's own headquarters, stunned silence fell.
Celeste stared at the monitor.
Her face went pale.

"No…" she whispered.

She lunged—striking Mira, screaming. Another gunshot rang out.

The window behind them shattered.

A thousand shards exploded outward.

Wind howled in, cold and blinding.

The women staggered, wind tearing at hair and clothing, alarms screaming. Mira's boots skidded on blood-slick glass as she tried to brace herself.

Celeste turned, wild-eyed, raising the gun toward the console—

And Mira tackled her.

They crashed into the shattered frame, glass cutting deep. Celeste lost her grip—her weapon went spinning into the wind. Both women tumbled against the jagged edge of the broken window.

Celeste slipped.

Mira caught her wrist just in time.

She held on, fingers bloodied, legs braced. Fifty stories below, the city glistened like a broken promise. The wind tore at them both.

Their eyes met.

Celeste dangled, her mouth slack with disbelief. "What have you done?" she whispered.

Mira's arm shook with the effort. "What was necessary," she said.

Celeste blinked. For a moment, the fire went out of her. Her weight shifted—and Mira heaved.

She pulled her enemy back to safety.

Celeste collapsed onto the floor, gasping, defeated. She didn't resist. She didn't speak. The power was gone from her.

Behind them, the screens still blazed.

Jonah limped toward Mira, kicking the fallen pistol aside. His breath came in shallow gulps. "You did it," he said, awe soft in his voice.

Mira looked past him, eyes on the monitors.

Messages poured in. Names. Dates. Locations. Stories. Grief. Fury.

Memories, surfacing at last.

People remembering.

People believing.

People *waking up.*

Across the tower, alarms still howled. Security forces scrambled. The world was breaking wide open.

But Mira felt something she hadn't felt in years.

Hope.

Celeste remained on the floor, hollowed, her empire burning from the inside.

And through the broken window, dawn finally arrived.

Sunlight poured over the city—bruised and battered, but still standing.

Mira, arm bleeding, limbs shaking, stood tall in the golden light.

The truth was free.

And the world would never forget again.

14

Uprising of Memory

By dawn, the city was breathing again.
Not in calm.
But in truth.

Mira stood at the top of the Unity Tower's spiral stairwell, hand pressed against the glass, watching the horizon burn from a rusted orange into streaks of fragile, tentative blue. For so long, SkyShield had dyed the sky a colorless dusk, muting sunrises into gray smudges. But now—just barely— the light broke through. It didn't feel like a miracle. It felt like a beginning.

She had imagined the aftermath would be still. Silent.

It wasn't.

It was alive.

Beneath her, the streets swelled with the rhythm of rebellion. The curfew had collapsed like a dam, and the people had flooded forward to fill the vacuum. They surged through alleys and boulevards, barefoot and bandaged, still in pajamas, still in hospital gowns, still clutching their forgotten names. Some held candles. Others held hastily scrawled signs: **WE REMEMBER.**

RELEASE THE CURE. MEMORY IS POWER. NO MORE LIES.

A tide had turned.

And this time, it wasn't receding.

Mira and Jonah wove through the chaos, weary and half-limping, sweat and blood still drying on their clothes. Jonah's brow was wrapped in gauze; Mira's left arm was stiff and burning from where Celeste's bullet had grazed her. But adrenaline kept them upright. Something deeper kept them moving.

Everywhere they looked, people were waking up—not just from sleep, but from forgetting.

Some cried out in joy as they recognized a loved one in the crowd. Others sank to their knees in sobs, clutching memory logs or the photos they had carried like relics. A woman fell to the ground in front of Mira, holding a crumpled family portrait to her chest. "They told me my daughter never existed," she said through trembling lips. "They made me believe it was a dream."

Drones buzzed overhead.

But they didn't issue commands.

Some simply hovered, camera lights off. Others flickered and drifted down, confused, unpowered—disabled by their own engineers, perhaps, or by those who had finally chosen the people over the code.

Even the soldiers had changed.

Mira watched in disbelief as black-clad guards at the perimeter of Civic Square stood motionless, weapons held low. One removed his helmet—a young man, barely twenty, cheeks streaked with tears. He looked at Mira, straight through the exhaustion and blood on her face, and said simply:

"Thank you."

The moment held—suspended in time—before others began lowering their weapons, one by one.

And then she saw it.

At the foot of the Unity Tower steps, flanked by a ring of silent guards, stood Celeste Drake. Her hands were cuffed in front of her, the pristine uniform rumpled, the ministerial pin stripped from her lapel. Her eyes were hollow. Her chin lifted in forced dignity, but the weight of betrayal sagged her spine.

Her own elite guard led her away.

She wasn't resisting.

The crowd parted as she passed, a wave of silence falling over them. Some hurled curses. Others simply stared. But no one moved to harm her. That part of the world—the part ruled by fear—had ended in the control room hours ago.

Mira stepped forward.

Their eyes met, across the bodies, the banners, the debris of revolution.

There was no anger left in Celeste. Only defeat. And, perhaps, a sliver of grudging respect. As if, in Mira, she saw what she could never be—what she had once imagined herself becoming before compromise consumed her.

She didn't speak.

Neither did Mira.

There was nothing left to say between them.

Only truth.

Only history.

But there was still one name echoing through Mira's bones like thunder.

Lena.

79

She turned to Jonah, heart pounding anew. "We have to find her—*now.*"

Jonah didn't hesitate. "I've got access to Ministry databases through the broadcast breach—we'll trace every quarantine transfer log."

With systems still flickering in and out across the grid, it took every backdoor code Jonah knew and a few he improvised. After what felt like an eternity, a line of text confirmed what Mira had feared: **Lena Solis – Sector D: Medical Quarantine.**

A memory cage.

A clinical prison where patients deemed "high-risk degenerates" were isolated, monitored, forgotten.

They ran.

Through corridors still echoing with alarms. Down boulevards turned battleground. Across barricades being dismantled by laughing citizens. Mira barely felt her injuries anymore. Her breath burned. Her muscles screamed. But she ran like fire.

And then—Sector D.

The doors slid open with a groan.

The ward inside was eerily still.

Patients blinked beneath harsh lights. Some clutched bedframes. Others wandered. Nurses rushed between them, trying to explain what was happening, weeping as they delivered the news: *You are not alone anymore. You are not crazy. The truth is real.*

And at the far end—

Lena.

Hunched on a cot. Hair tangled, lips murmuring something Mira couldn't hear. Knees drawn up to her chest. Her eyes vacant. Searching the air for something lost.

Mira's voice shattered the silence.

"**Lena!**"

Her sister looked up, slow and dazed. "I… know you, don't I?"

Mira dropped to her knees beside the cot, took Lena's hands in hers. They were cold, and shaking.

"It's me," Mira said, choking on tears. "It's Mira. I came back. Like I promised. I'm here."

Lena blinked rapidly. "I try to remember," she whispered. "But it slips. I forget. I don't want to, but I do."

Mira leaned forward, brushing sweaty strands from her sister's face. Her voice cracked, but she began to sing:

"Duérmete niña, duérmete ya,

que viene el cuco y te llevará…"

The lullaby. Their mother's song.

Lena froze.

Then, slowly—so slowly—her lips began to move. Wordlessly at first. Then she sang the next line.

"Duérmete niña, duérmete ya…"

Her eyes cleared.

And she whispered, "**Mira.**"

They collapsed into each other, sobbing. Clinging like shipwreck survivors pulled from the tide.

A gentle voice interrupted. A young doctor stood beside them, face haggard with exhaustion but eyes warm.

Mira held out the vial.

"Elena Alvarez made this. It's the antidote. Can you—can you give it to her?"

The doctor examined it, nodded. "We've started full trials already. The rollout's begun. We'll take care of her now."

As the injection slid into Lena's arm, Mira kissed her forehead.

"You're going to remember everything," she whispered. "You're going to be okay."

And for the first time in years, she believed it.

Outside, the world had cracked open.

And something green was growing through.

Ministry labs had been raided. Antidote caches liberated. Scientists freed from hidden blacksites. And at the center of it all, Dr. Elena Alvarez—bruised, limping, but smiling—stood once again at the helm of something she could be proud of.

She and Mira embraced in the hallway outside the ward.

Neither spoke for a long moment.

Then Mira said, "You made it."

Elena smiled faintly. "We made it."

In the streets, citizens and doctors worked side by side.

Vials were passed like communion.

Elders held hands with children. Strangers shared memory fragments, writing them in handmade booklets—Memory Logs—bound with string, passed from person to person. "Your name." "Your favorite song." "Who you once loved."

Even amidst the noise, there was reverence.

The world was remembering itself.

And rewriting it at the same time.

As the morning sun climbed, something beautiful happened on the wall beside the now-abandoned Ministry.

A mural.

New. Massive. Brilliant.

It showed a human brain unfurling like a flower—each petal a different color, alive with energy. Neurons blossoming into stars.

And beneath it, just one word:

TRUTH.

Mira stood beneath it, hand in Jonah's, her sister resting nearby beneath a warm blanket, dozing in safety.

The city around her was scarred. Ruined.

But it was *awake.*

And that was enough.

The war for memory was over.

And the world had chosen to remember.

15

A New Dawn

Weeks had passed, though sometimes Mira still startled awake expecting sirens, shouting, the hard metal slam of lockdown doors.

Instead, she rose to birdsong. Real birdsong.

It was tentative, brittle as blown glass, but it was real. The kind of quiet that used to exist only in old poems or the final pages of fairy tales. She lay in bed some mornings, eyes open, afraid to believe it was lasting. That it wouldn't be snatched away like so much else had been.

But outside, the city—her city—was still breathing. Shaky, scarred, but alive.

The world hadn't healed overnight. The air still carried the haze of smoke and the sharp edge of SkyShield's remnants. Rain was still acid-tinged some days. Crops were erratic. The storms hadn't stopped coming.

But now… at last… the truth had room to breathe.

The Unity regime collapsed swiftly in the wake of the broadcast. The flood of evidence had been undeniable—Celeste's voice, the buried data, the cruel calculus of who was allowed to remember and who was left to vanish inside themselves. The people had risen not with vengeance, but with clarity.

Truth had become its own kind of revolution.

A provisional council had taken the reins: doctors, archivists, old civil servants who had quietly resisted, and young leaders whose families had vanished under the old regime. They stood beneath banners that no longer bore Unity's blank circle. Their oaths were not to dominion, but to transparency. To memory. To care.

No more secrets. No more scapegoats. No more forgetting.

And then—miraculously—aid came.

Real aid.

Nations long locked out by Unity's paranoid isolation began to send food, medicine, engineers. Old channels reopened. Volunteers from across the world arrived—bringing seeds, clean water technologies, books. Books! Mira helped unpack a shipment from India that included children's picture stories and preserved oral histories on wax cylinders. She cried over them. Held them to her chest.

The veil had lifted.

The world, it seemed, remembered how to care.

Mira found herself transformed.

Not a fugitive. Not a fighter. Not even a symbol.

She had become something else.

A **historian**.

She now led the **Community Archive of Remembrance**, headquartered inside the very building that once housed the Ministry's records—the same place she'd once digitized redacted headlines under flickering lights and fear.

Now it hummed with purpose. With life.

The Archive was open every day. No gates. No passwords. The halls of censorship had been reborn as chambers of healing. Where once protest records had been erased, now music played: old folk recordings, oral testimonies, readings of restored letters.

There were no blacked-out documents now.

No erased names.

In Mira's Archive, truth was not a liability. It was sacred.

She launched a project called **Memory Drives**—a citywide call for recovered artifacts. Every day, citizens arrived with armfuls of salvaged history: crumpled photos from flooded drawers, corrupted flash sticks containing fragments of old journals, fragments of school essays, recipes written in half-faded pencil.

Volunteers scanned, restored, labeled, and, whenever possible, helped return them to their original owners.

Some items had no match. Those were kept in the central gallery—a living museum of memory. Each artifact tagged with a note: **"Belongs to someone. Please claim if you remember."**

Every recovery was a resurrection.

One golden afternoon, Mira stood in the Archive's rotunda, hand resting on the centerpiece exhibit.

A glass case held her father's weathered journal—its spine cracked, pages soft from water damage. Beside it sat a sealed folder stamped in brittle ink: *Project SkyShield—Internal Reports.* A small bronze plaque beneath read:

Dr. Carlo Solis – A Voice That Remembered.

Mira touched the glass.

"I told you I'd protect it," she whispered. "And I did."

By her side, Lena sat sketching on a digital tablet. Her lines were confident again. Her laugh, unguarded. She was stronger now. Still healing, still forgetful some days—but laughter returned more easily. Memory came back in sparks. In color.

"I remember the lake," Lena said suddenly. "We went there when I was seven. I lost my shoe in the mud."

Mira smiled, tears rising. "You cried for hours."

"I did not," Lena said, grinning wide. "I… maybe for one hour."

They laughed together. And it sounded like sunlight.

Later that week, Mira walked alone to the Memorial Wall in the Civic Plaza.

Once, this had been Unity's central propaganda stage—giant screens blaring lies in every direction. Now it was quiet. Peaceful.

A garden had replaced the concrete. The air was heavy with lavender and rosemary. Between the flowers stood a curved stone wall, engraved with names.

Mira ran her fingers across two of them.

Isabel Solis.

Carlo Solis.

"Mamá… Papá…"

She closed her eyes, whispered the words like a prayer.

"I still dream of him," she said aloud, and felt Jonah step beside her. "Sometimes we're in the kitchen. He's making arepas. Reading from some old chemistry book. And he remembers everything. My name. The answers. He says he's proud."

Jonah took her hand, gave it a gentle squeeze.

"He would be," he said. "So would she."

They stood quietly together as other visitors came and went. Some left flowers. Others left tiny totems: old bookmarks, faded ID badges, toy soldiers. A child tucked a picture of her grandfather into the wall's base.

No one forgot alone anymore.

All across the city, restoration bloomed in strange, beautiful ways.

Children chalked drawings beside rain-harvesting tanks. Families gathered for community cooking circles, trading old recipes brought back from memory logs. Neighbors taught one another how to mend clothes, how to bake bread, how to fix things.

There were dance classes in the old underground train stations. Poetry readings in the clinic waiting rooms. Murals of before and after—faces that had been blurred now painted sharp and bold on the sides of buildings.

Memory clinics became meeting houses. People sat in circles, taking turns sharing moments they thought were gone forever.

The scars were still there. The pain had not vanished.

But it had been named. And once named, it could be shared. And once shared... it could begin to heal.

That evening, Mira and Jonah walked beneath lanterns strung across the city square.

The plaza that had once displayed the towering Unity statue— looming, blank-eyed, flanked by surveillance drones—was now transformed.

That metal colossus had been melted down. The metal repurposed.

In its place now stood a sculpture.

Simple, profound.

Two hands, interlocked, rising from the earth—one smooth, the other cracked and weathered. Around the base of the statue, names were etched into stone like roots—thousands of them: victims of the climate disasters, of the Forgetting, of silence.

Out of the hands grew sculpted vines and flowers, climbing upward in bloom.

A plaque beneath read:

"To those who were lost.

To those who remembered.

To those who rebuilt."

Mira stood beside it at sunrise, Lena tucked into her side under a shared blanket.

She watched the first golden rays stretch across rooftops, catch on windows, flicker across green leaves and new brick. It painted the statue, lit up the vines, shimmered on the names.

And for the first time in Mira's life, it didn't feel like a warning.

It felt like a beginning.

She closed her eyes and breathed in.

I won't let the world forget again, she promised, silently. *Not what we lost. Not what we learned. Not who we are.*

Memory, she understood now, wasn't just sorrow.

It was proof.

Of love. Of legacy.

Of survival.

The first full light of morning touched her face.

The city stirred around her.

A new day had begun.

And this time—

The world would remember.

— **End** —

16

Conclusion

In the end, *Where the World Forgets* is not just a dystopian tale of collapse and control—it's a testament to the enduring power of truth, memory, and love.

Mira's journey from grief-stricken survivor to truth-bearer is a mirror for all of us living in uncertain times. Her choice—to risk everything for the sake of remembering—echoes beyond her world. It asks us, too, to choose courage over comfort, integrity over silence.

Though the scars of catastrophe remain, the story closes with the possibility of healing—not because the world is suddenly whole, but because its people are finally *awake*. The light of truth, once buried, now shines into every corner.

Through collective memory, families are made whole again. Through restored history, justice begins. And through one girl's refusal to forget, humanity remembers who it is.

As you turn the final page, may you carry this:

That memory is not weakness, but strength.

That telling the truth is a radical act of hope.

And that no matter how dark the sky becomes, there is always a dawn worth rising for.

Never stop remembering.

Never stop telling the stories that matter.

Epilogue

The city breathes differently now.

Where once sirens wailed and silence ruled, there are songs—soft ones, uncertain, but real. On the steps of the old Ministry building, children draw with chalk: spirals, suns, names. Some of the names are new. Some are remembered.

Mira walks the streets with Lena beside her. They carry journals, not weapons. Stories, not secrets. The Archive of Remembrance hums with life, filled with voices once thought lost. Each recovered letter, each photo pinned to the walls, is a thread sewn back into the tapestry of a fractured world.

Lena's laughter rings out as she describes a dream she had—of their parents, young and dancing. Mira smiles, eyes glistening. The dream is new, but the feeling is old, and real. Memory, she's learned, isn't just what happened. It's what *matters*.

Jonah meets them at the plaza, his sleeves rolled up, hands dirt-streaked from helping plant another garden. He doesn't need to speak. The way his hand finds Mira's says everything.

Together, they make their way to the monument—no longer a statue to power, but to pain, truth, and the will to heal. Around them, people light candles. Others read names aloud. The wind carries stories like seeds.

And as the sun rises—gentle, golden, *promising*—Mira closes her eyes.

She remembers.

The fear.

The cost.

The courage.

The fire.

But more than anything, she remembers *the choice*—and that in choosing truth, she gave the world its memory back.

When she opens her eyes, the city stands before her—not perfect, not healed, but alive.

This is not the end.

It is the beginning of everything worth remembering.

We survived the forgetting.
Now we begin to remember—together.

Afterword

Stories are powerful because they help us remember—who we are, where we've been, and what we've lost along the way. *Where the World Forgets* began as a fictional exploration of a dystopian future, but it quickly became something more intimate and urgent: a reflection on truth, memory, and the fragile bonds that hold us together.

Writing this book was, in many ways, an act of remembering. Remembering that the fight for truth is never easy. That love, even when fractured by time or trauma, endures. And that even the quietest voice can shift the course of history if it refuses to be silenced.

Mira's journey is one of transformation—from sorrow to strength, from silence to speech. Her bravery is not without cost, but it reminds us that **redemption is real**, and that the truth, once spoken, cannot be unspoken.

As you close this book, I hope you carry its message with you:

That memory is not just personal—it is political.

That stories can heal what systems have broken.

And that when we dare to remember, we also dare to rebuild.

In a world that too often asks us to forget, may you be the one who remembers.

Thank you for walking this path with Mira.

Thank you for not looking away.

With gratitude,

— Abdellatif Raji

Bonus Scene – "The Memory Garden"

Set six months after the end of the novel.

Mira knelt in the soil beneath a morning sky brushed with pale clouds, her fingers deep in the dirt. The garden was quiet today—only the soft hum of pollinators and the whisper of leaves above. Rows of memory blossoms stretched before her: not literal flowers, but reclaimed stories planted like seeds.

Every plant was paired with a story: a small tag in waterproof ink told the tale.

A rosebush tended by a man who remembered how to sing lullabies in three languages.

A sprouting fig tree, donated in honor of a lost sister who once dreamed of living on Mars.

A patch of sweet basil that had helped a boy remember the taste of his grandmother's soup.

Mira reached for a young sunflower growing stubbornly near the edge of the fence. She pressed the soil gently around its roots. A small laminated card fluttered beside it, attached with twine.

"In memory of Roland Vera. Mechanic. Friend. Gave my water filter a second life. Forgot his name—but not his kindness."

She smiled softly.

From the path, Lena called out, "You're going to miss the ceremony!"

Mira brushed dirt from her hands and stood. Jonah was already there, adjusting the amplifier. Children gathered, their arms full of hand-written story scrolls. It was the first **Annual Remembrance Day**. A holiday not about war or victory—but about remembering those who couldn't. Those who were stolen.

Mira stepped to the podium.

"Before we begin," she said into the mic, her voice carrying over the garden, "I want to thank each of you—for keeping the memories alive. For planting what was nearly lost. You've all proven what my father once said: that memory is more than survival. It's how we become human again."

Lena passed her a flower.

A memory rose.

Mira placed it beside the statue in the garden's center. Its base read:

"For those who forgot. For those who remembered for them."

The petals gleamed gold in the light.

Author's Note – On Memory, Truth, and Hope

Dear Reader,

The Memory Plague began, for me, with a single haunting question:

> *What would happen if we started forgetting not just names and dates—but our shared truth?*

In writing Mira's story, I wasn't just imagining a dystopian future. I was writing about *now*—about our relationship with memory, truth, and the fragile ways we record what matters. In an age of disinformation, climate anxiety, and fractured communities, the ability to hold onto our collective memory becomes a revolutionary act.

Mira was never meant to be a chosen one. She's a sister. A daughter. An archivist clinging to books in a world that prefers silence. Her superpower is *persistence*. Her resistance is *remembrance*. Through her eyes, I wanted to explore how memory is not just a personal experience—it's a moral compass, a call to action, a form of resistance.

The Forgetting in this novel isn't just a plot device. It's a metaphor for all the ways societies erase inconvenient truths: environmental warnings, historical atrocities, the quiet heroism of ordinary people. The antidote, then, is not just medicine. It's *awareness*. It's courage. It's the act of telling the truth, even when it hurts.

I hope this story moved you.

And more than that—I hope it reminded you to *remember*.

With gratitude and fire,

Abdellatif Raji

Personal Reflection – The Autodidact's Journey

As an autodidact—someone who learns outside formal systems—I've always believed stories are one of the purest ways to educate, to question, to connect. I didn't study literature in a university. I didn't take writing workshops. I built this story piece by piece through late-night research, obsessive reading, and relentless love for language.

This novel was my syllabus. My test. My thesis.

And you, dear reader, are the graduation.

I hope *The Memory Plague* reminded you of the stories that shaped *you*—the ones that live in dusty notebooks, old letters, or the way your grandmother used to hum when she cooked. Stories aren't just something we consume. They're something we carry, like satchels full of maps and old photographs, through every storm we survive.

Thank you for carrying this one with me.

Please—never stop remembering.

And never stop writing your own.

— With hope,

Abdellatif Raji

About the Author

Abdellatif Raji is an autodidact—*a lifelong learner forged by curiosity, not classrooms*. With no formal degree in literature or creative writing, he built his voice from dog-eared library books, midnight scribbles, and a relentless hunger to understand the world.

His education came from the margins: from whispered stories passed down in families, from underground forums, from listening deeply to those rarely heard. He believes that knowledge is not a privilege but a birthright—and that storytelling is one of humanity's oldest and most radical forms of truth-telling.

Where the World Forgets is his debut novel, born from sleepless nights, real-world anxieties, and a defiant belief that one voice—however untrained or imperfect—*can matter*.

When not writing, Raji can be found sketching wild ideas in coffee-stained notebooks, wandering city streets with a secondhand camera, or helping others uncover their own stories—because everyone has one.

This book, like its author, was self-taught, self-built, and written with the kind of hope that refuses to be forgotten.

You can connect with me on:
🌐 https://www.abdellatifraji.com

Subscribe to my newsletter:
✉ https://www.wheretheworldforgets.com